SECONDS

DAVID ELY

SECONDS

The Cult Classic Novel

HARPER Voyager

An Imprint of HarperCollins Publishers

A print edition of *Seconds* was originally published in August 1964 by Signet, a division of Random House, Inc.

EPub Edition JANUARY 2013 ISBN: 9780062264923

Print Edition ISBN: 9780062264930

10 9 8 7 6 5 4 3 2 1

To Peggy

CHAPTER 1

It was noon. Time to go. He stood up behind his desk, thinking that this would probably be the last time he would stand there, the last time he would cross his office to pick up his hat, and the last time he would open that door with the frosted pane which bore his name and title.

In the outer office, he paused beside his secretary's desk.

"I'll probably be a little late getting back from lunch. It's such a fine day, I may take a walk."

"Yes, sir."

He turned and proceeded toward the great glass wall that marked the Broadway side of the bank. Be casual, he told himself. Be ordinary. Remember, you're just going out to lunch. But it occurred to him that he did not have the vaguest notion of how to counterfeit the act of going out to lunch. Was there a special way of walking? Did one saunter or rush out hungrily or what? He had gone out to lunch every working day for more than twenty-five years, and yet now, when he had to pretend to do it, he was baffled.

On Broadway, he paused deliberately to sniff the air and eye the crowds. He supposed this was the kind of thing he usually did on those days when he was going out alone to eat. Something to show how unhurried he was, and that he was of sufficient rank not to worry about the precise time of his return.

He glanced around at the wall of glass. It did not seem quite possible that he was really never going back. The idea might be no more substantial than the exhaust that rose up from the traffic on the street, for the sun to burn away. Surely, if he were in earnest, then his demeanor would have been visibly agitated during the past few days. His associates would have divined his intentions, and at any moment they would come rushing out to seize him, with cries of: "Good Lord, man—you can't be thinking of doing *that!*"

It was amusing. Almost. Ah, it was easy enough to slip away prosaically during an ordinary lunch hour— but the rest of it . . . ! He was not at all sure where he would be going. He knew why, and he had a fairly good idea of what would be awaiting him, but he was not certain where it might be. It would be, he suspected, a complicated process. He had an address on the lower East Side, written on a scrap of paper that looked as if it had been used over and over, many times, but that would probably be only the beginning.

Again he wondered whether he should go. He had decided to go, true enough, and yet a decision no one else knew about was easily withdrawn. So easily, in fact, that there was some doubt whether it amounted to a decision at all. For another thing, his mood was wrong. He was too calm. One did not do this sort of thing without some internal evidence of emotion. Perhaps his calmness was a signal that he was not really intending to go through with it, after all.

Yet he hailed a taxi anyway and when the driver asked where to go, he drew the scrap of paper from his pocket and read the address aloud.

In ten minutes, he had alighted and was standing on a sidewalk under the inspection of men in shabby jackets and weathered caps who edged around him, eyeing his grey tailored suit, his spotless shoes, and most of all, his Homburg.

He damned them back with his banker's eyes. He was troubled and annoyed, for the address was that of a tailor shop, grey with steam from a great pressing machine. He hesitated irritably at the door, thinking that there must be some mistake. For a moment he considered turning away, although he suspected that he had by now gone too far to retreat without losing his chance forever. The people he sought had made it clear that they could not afford to have fainthearted clients.

He stepped inside. At least he would go this far. If the trail were false and ended here, so be it.

A short, elderly man with bunched cheek muscles stood up behind the counter.

"Yah?"

"Good afternoon. My name—" he could not help a slight hesitation "—is Wilson." He held out the scrap of paper. "Perhaps you can help me."

The old man did not take the paper. He barely looked at it. He stared at his visitor. "Yah?"

"I was given this address. Is tailoring all you do?"

"We clean and press, mister."

"I don't mean that."

But he was sure now. He was sure because none of the other men working there had stopped to examine him. A quick look or two, that was all. And certainly, if this were an ordinary tailor shop, the sight of a robust, greying gentleman wearing a Homburg would be worth attention. There was but one reasonable explanation: other prosperous gentlemen, similarly attired, must have preceded him from time to time, and the workmen were under orders not to gape.

The old tailor seemed to have finished his study of the suit, the florid face, and the Homburg.

"Yah, well, I guess it's another place you want. They moved out of here last year."

The man who called himself Wilson waited confidently. The old man lied, of course. They employed him as a scout, to give advance warning by telephone of any caller who seemed suspicious. It appeared unduly secretive, and yet doubtless they had ample reason to be careful.

"Here's where it is. I got it wrote down."

"Thank you very much."

It was another scrap of paper, quite like the first. Wilson glanced at it and tucked it into his pocket.

"Goodbye," he said.

"Yah."

He walked along the street toward an intersection, to flag a taxi. The back of his neck itched, as if the old tailor's gaze were tickling it, and he felt a slight chill— unaccountable, for the day was warm and he was actually perspiring.

He patted his face with his handkerchief. Ah, he thought, why not give it up? Go back to the office. Forget about it. That little chill—it might mean a fever. He ought to consider his health. In any case, he was too old for this sort of thing. Five years ago, perhaps, he could have managed it.

"Taxi!"

He raised his arm commandingly and a cruising cab swerved obediently toward the curb.

Behind him there was a derisive laugh. Startled, he turned and saw a youth and a girl lounging arm in arm against a building. The young man, sneering at him openly, made a boorish remark about the Homburg.

Fortunately the cab had arrived. Wilson stepped in and slammed the door. Such an impertinence would never have happened on Wall Street. Perhaps it served him right for wandering about parts of the city where there were young hoodlums instead of respectful little clerks.

"Where to, mister?"

"Oh." He found that he held the second scrap of

paper in his hand and that he was reading the address aloud. The insulting behavior of that youth had rattled him, evidently. Even so, it would not be too late to turn back to the office which he had, so tentatively, abandoned less than an hour before.

The second address proved to be that of a dilapidated warehouse near the fish market, an odorous area filled with giant trucks and strewn with refuse.

"You sure this is what you want, mister?"

Habit answered: "Of course." Wilson was not accustomed to make mistakes.

He got out in front of a battered door marked "Office." The driver waited, presumably for his fare to admit his error and climb back in.

Annoyed by the driver's presumption, Wilson did not hesitate, but peremptorily twisted the knob and stepped inside. It was a badly lighted place, where dusty boxes were haphazardly stacked, and it smelled, not unpleasantly, of ink.

"Hello there!"

He looked around, impatiently searching for someone to report to. The dust bothered him; he fretted lest it smudge his suit. If he were actually going back to the bank, it would be vexing to have to daub at his clothing with a dampened handkerchief, and besides, old Mr. Franks, the senior vice president, would be bound to call him in about some trifle or other, and Mr. Franks looked at one's personal appearance with an examiner's eye.

"Ah, Mr. Wilson!" From the dim interior of the

warehouse hurried the figure of a bulky man, bald as an onion. He hastily completed the process of wiping his hands with a paper towel and thrust the towel into his hip pocket. "I'm sorry, sir, to have kept you waiting. But—" He cleared his throat apologetically. From a distance came the lugubrious sound of a toilet filling.

"Quite all right," said Wilson, coldly. He looked with distaste around the little office, which merged on an uncertain basis with the larger spread of the main section of the warehouse. "Surely, this isn't—"

"Oh, no." The bulky man smiled in apology. Then, with a worried look, he went hastily to a window. "Your taxi, sir, it's still . . . Ah, *now* it's going. That's good." He turned and inclined his head deferentially. "No, sir. We have one more stop to make, sir."

"We both go?"

"I'm your guide, Mr. Wilson." The man was dressed in dungarees and a blue shirt, which was stained with perspiration. His white arms, bared to the elbows, were muscularly thick, and his hands were ridged with calluses, but his manner suggested that he had spent many years as someone's butler or valet.

He glanced at Wilson's suit. "We, um, go as workmen, sir. I'm afraid you'll have to slip a coverall over your clothing, sir, and exchange your hat for a cap."

Wilson stirred suspiciously.

"I know it sounds unnecessary, sir," the man went on, "but we must go in through a delivery entrance. It's a precaution, sir. You don't want to be recognized going in, because . . ." He cleared his throat and smiled appeasingly. "Because you won't be coming out, sir. That is, you won't be *seen* coming out. It's an inconvenience, Mr. Wilson. You're right about that. But only a minor one, sir. And temporary."

"Well, all right."

"Very good, sir."

The man hastened off into the main part of the warehouse. In a few moments, he returned carrying a large stained coverall formally over one arm, holding the collar with his other hand, as if the garment were an evening suit.

"This should fit you well enough, sir."

Wilson stepped into the capacious legs of the coverall, and adjusted the upper portion to his arms and shoulders.

"Your hat, sir."

He passed the Homburg to the bald man and received a cloth cap to wear.

"And, if you don't mind, Mr. Wilson, a little dust on your face."

"Eh?"

"If you could rub a little dust on your face. You look too cleanly for your new outfit, sir . . . Very good, sir. That's quite enough . . . If you would follow me, sir?"

They walked into the interior of the warehouse, wary of the heaps of grimy cartons.

Wilson tried to joke, to cover his sense of indignity. "I must say I, um, feel like a character in a play, or something."

"It *is* unusual, sir," the respectful voice replied.

"Yes, all the gentlemen are rather taken aback by this part of it, I must say, and I don't blame them."

The shape of a truck appeared in the shadows.

"Have you . . . escorted many gentlemen, then?"

"Quite a few, sir. Let me just get these doors open—" The bald man grunted as he forced the handle up and pulled the double rear doors apart. "If you wouldn't mind stepping inside, Mr. Wilson. There's a sort of bench along one side. You'll be comfortable enough for a short ride, I think."

"Wouldn't it be better if I rode up front, beside you?"

"The gentlemen are asked to ride in the back, sir, I'm afraid."

"I see." Wilson pursed his lips. If the man's attitude had been in the least abrupt, he would have refused; but as it was, the request seemed modest enough. "All right, then."

He swung himself up, gasping from the unaccustomed effort. "Oh, my hat."

"I have it, sir."

"Well, all right."

"Very good, Mr. Wilson."

The doors swung shut. There was a rasp and a click as the handle snapped down, and Wilson, feeling his way toward the bench, realized that he was, in effect, locked in. There was no window, either. He was penned up like a steer. It occurred to him that he should protest. An important client should hardly submit to being hauled around the city in such an unseemly fashion. It set a bad precedent for subsequent relationships. But on the other hand, he reflected, he had clambered into the truck voluntarily, and he could not now demand to be let out without risking . . . well, risking refusal, for that deferential guide of his would undoubtedly keep him there, lacking the requisite authority to do otherwise. The man had his orders, after all.

The engine rumbled. The truck moved slowly forward, and Wilson, leaning back for support against the joggling motion, realized that his position had become, almost against his will, more and more ambiguous. First, he had set out by taxi without seriously intending to do more than inspect the premises at the initial address—at least, it seemed that those had been his intentions—and then he had somehow entered the tailor shop, and although he subsequently had determined to return to the office, it had been almost by a perverse little accident—the jeering of that young criminal—that he had been flustered into going to the second address; and now, having acquiesced in the courteous instructions of his guide, without really having given adequate thought to what might be involved, here he was wearing a cloth cap and a dirty coverall, with his face smudged by dust.

Oh well, having gone this far, he decided, it would be foolish not to follow through with it, at least to the point where his curiosity would be satisfied. That would take perhaps an hour or so, at the most. Then he could stop somewhere to wash up, and return at his leisure to the bank. It would all make a good story—

although he would be unable to tell it, of course. Yes, that was the way to look at it; not that he had somehow gotten himself into a cap and coverall and locked into a truck bound for Lord knew where, but that he was having a bit of diversion on his lunch hour.

It was not an unpleasant ride. For the first time in years, Wilson experienced the sensation of irresponsibility. Shut up in darkness the way he was, he clearly had no control over the immediate events which affected him, and he decided, with surprising readiness, not to bother about them. Did they transport all of their clients this way—in effect, blindfolded—in order to keep their location a secret? Very well, if that's what they wanted. He did not care one way or the other. With his arms folded across his chest in quiet dignity, Wilson sat in repose, waiting.

"Mr. Wilson, sir—"

"Eh?"

"We're here, sir."

The bald man was peering inside. The rear doors were open again, and light was flowing in. Wilson rubbed his face and yawned, stretching himself awake from his brief nap.

The truck was parked in a narrow alley between towering buildings. There was nothing to distinguish this passage from a thousand others like it, and if indeed there had been some identifying marks, Wilson would not have had time to notice them, since his guide quickly but politely maneuvered him through an open doorway marked "Delivery."

"Very good, Mr. Wilson. We've done it." The guide seemed greatly relieved. "Now, sir, if you'll just follow the hall . . ."

The hallway ended in a circular room furnished in the manner of a physician's waiting room, with a sofa, a few chairs, and a table in the center where magazines were laid out. There were two doors side by side in the wall opposite the hallway entrance; one was marked "Staff Only." In a moment, a plain-faced young woman in a white uniform entered through this door, bearing a tray on which rested a cup and saucer and a sandwich on a plate.

"Mr. Wilson? There will be a short wait, I'm afraid. Perhaps you would like to have some refreshment."

She set the tray on top of the magazines.

"Yes, thank you," said Wilson. He glanced around for the guide, but the man had evidently completed his function, and his heavy figure was retreating down the hallway. However, Wilson was more interested in the contents of the tray, for he was accustomed to having had his lunch by this time, and so as soon as the young woman had withdrawn, he went to the table and ate the sandwich in quick bites, standing up. There was tea in the cup. He was mildly irked that the young woman had not supplied cream and sugar, but since she had gone and he was thirsty, he sipped it anyway. It was not too strong, although its aroma was strangely sour. Still, he imagined that it

would revive him from his sleepiness, so he drank it
down to the bottom.

Then he realized that he was still wearing the
coverall. That was no longer necessary, surely. He
unzipped it, pulled his arms and legs free of its encum-
bering folds, and, having retrieved his Homburg from
the sofa, where the guide had deposited it, felt much
more himself again, although he knew that his face
would still be dusty.

He frowned at his wristwatch. It was nearly a quarter to two. By the time he had met whoever it was that
would represent this firm, and had had an opportunity
to find out something about the operations involved
in the business, it would be much too late to return
to the office. He would need to call in, however. He
glanced about. There was no telephone in sight, not
even a receptionist, nothing but the two doors, which
he had better not go wandering through, for fear of
being absent when they called for him.

No matter. He selected a magazine and sat down on
the sofa to wait. Oddly enough, the tea had not perked
him up at all, for he felt drowsier than ever, and fell to
yawning almost uncontrollably. For a few moments he
resisted what was rapidly becoming an overwhelming
urge to sleep, and then he slumped back to accept what
seemed to be the inevitable demands of weariness.

There followed the most remarkable experience
of his life. At the time, and immediately thereafter, it
seemed to be a dream, but a dream of the utmost clarity, and with disturbing physical sensations of reality.

His head ached with a steady pain, and his vision was peculiarly affected, for although he witnessed the events which took place, everything appeared to occur in a milky vapor, as if his eyes were literally clouded.

First, unseen persons helped him to his feet and ushered him out of the waiting room into what seemed to be a boudoir, dominated by a massive four-poster bed. He could not see the entire room, for he felt unable to turn his head, but he did not think there was a window, which seemed to him as odd as the fact that a bedroom would adjoin the waiting room.

As he stood surveying what lay before him, lights began to blink at him and he heard the murmur of voices nearby, although he could see no one, and despite his preoccupation with his headache he thought he detected fingers plucking at his clothing, and hands jostling him slightly this way and that. Even so, he not only was powerless to move of his own accord, but also was without the desire to do so, and blankly accepted the fingers, hands, voices, and lights as further properties of what he imagined to be a dream.

The bed drew closer. He seemed to be at its very edge. He perceived that it was not empty, but was in fact occupied by a woman, sleeping with her hair flared exquisitely over a white pillow.

The woman stirred. Her eyelids fluttered. They opened, and she sat up slowly, with an expression at first puzzled, then worried, and finally, as she turned her head to face him fully, horrified. She screamed—or, rather, seemed to scream, for although her mouth gaped open and her throat muscles strained, he heard no sound.

Dream or not, he thought it best to placate her. He tried to utter words, in vain; he sought to raise his hand in a peaceable gesture, but his arm remained motionless. At the same time he found himself still closer to the bed, as if he were being propelled there by some hidden force, so that soon he was virtually bending over the woman, who continued to shriek silently, her eyes rolling in terror. He himself was not the least perturbed, which he accepted as additional evidence that the woman, the room, and everything associated with it were only the creations of his mind.

However, he was somewhat taken aback to see that her nightgown was being methodically shredded by a pair of hands that were quite probably his own, and soon the woman's body was revealed to the impropriety of his examination. It was, he discovered, a remarkably lush body, slightly plump, with the armpits and pubic area cleanly shaven. It—or rather the woman— wriggled before him now in nakedness, and although he felt distinctly uncomfortable, he seemed unable to do other than remain as he was, leaning attentively over her.

It appeared that he had leaned too far. He lost his balance and toppled slowly onto the woman, and as he did so, the contact of her flesh indicated that he, too, was unclothed. Her soundless screams continued. She labored beneath him, but strangely enough, although it seemed that she was attempting to repulse him, she was actually clasping him closer, frustrating his efforts to twist aside. The lights of the room burned down more powerfully, and the murmur of voices there grew louder, as if a dozen idlers had wandered into his dream-bedroom to witness his disconcerting entanglement.

He began to question the validity of his experience as a dream. The fingers clawing at his back, the breasts that alternately caressed his chest and curved away, the smooth strong legs that turned against his own—these impressions were all too forcible to be the exhalation of the mind alone. His emotions were contradictory, as well. He was aware of a flicker of rage at being caught up in circumstances which could only embarrass him, and at the same time, he felt a remote sexual desire for the woman, whose perfumed limbs, writhing against his skin, evoked distant tinglings of passion.

The ferocity of the headache suddenly grew, intolerably. He heard himself cry out, he closed his eyes, he sank forward on the bed with a vision of grey circles spinning.

He awoke in an office. He was lying on a couch, his hands clasped on his stomach, his feet propped on a pillow, and his eyes fixed on a window that framed a delicate sunset behind a domino arrangement of tall buildings.

"Do you feel better, Mr. Wilson?"

The speaker was a tall gentleman of his own age,

dressed in an immaculate dark grey suit, who had moved into view beside the window, holding a pair of horn-rimmed spectacles in one hand.

"I believe I do, thank you."

Wilson resolved that he would not be hurried. He first ascertained that he was fully clothed in his own suit, then that his Homburg was resting on a low table beside the couch, and finally that his head was clear. He examined his physical sensations more closely. He felt empty, with no desire to do anything but remain as he was, lying down.

"You evidently had an attack of indigestion," the tall man remarked, calmly. "You had us a little worried, but we called a doctor and he said you would be quite all right, with a little rest. Are you sure you feel well enough to begin?"

"I suppose so."

Wilson reflected that he should commence questioning this gentleman rather sharply about the events of the afternoon. He took a deep breath, to test the functioning of his respiration, and finding it satisfactory, lowered his feet to the floor and sat up.

The office was one of those somewhat overmodernized establishments common to advertising agencies and similar enterprises whose executives must be prepared to make an impression of dash and efficiency on visiting clients. The desk was edged with two miniature dictaphones, an interoffice communications box, and a tiny file cabinet marked in gold letters: "Reddi-Ref." The cream-colored walls were bare, except for a pair of prints of English hunting scenes so small that they added to the atmosphere of efficiency, inasmuch as they clearly were not intended to attract the eye.

"My name is Joliffe," said Wilson's host, who was now leaning informally against the desk, swinging his spectacles in his hand. He touched a button on the desk. "What we say from now on will be recorded. I hope you don't mind."

"No, not at all," said Wilson. He thought for a moment and added: "I feel I should mind, but I don't." He glanced up, as if seeking some explanation for his remark.

Joliffe nodded, approvingly. "Right. Now, to start us off, I wonder if you would mind describing, to the best of your ability, your present state of mind. How do you feel at this moment, Mr. Wilson? Physically and mentally and emotionally?"

The question struck Wilson as being most appropriate, for he had been in the process of answering it, in his own mind, ever since he had awakened.

"I feel, um, rather convalescent," he began, concentrating deliberately, his brow wrinkled and his lips pursed. "I feel as if I'd recovered from some bender—though I rarely drink to excess—and everything seems . . . impersonal, unconnected with my usual habits of . . ." He hesitated, searching for the right words. Joliffe encouraged him with a patient and understanding nod. "My usual habits of thought and feeling," Wilson concluded.

"For example?"

"Well, for example, I should be quite anxious about the time. I realize that it's the end of the day, you see, and that I have been absent from the office without explanation, and that moreover my train is due to leave—" he regarded his watch "—in twenty minutes, but these facts seem to be unimportant. I know that I should call my superior at his home this evening without fail, to tell him why I did not return from lunch, and also I should telephone my wife to tell her that I will probably be arriving on a late train, or even that I plan to spend the night in town at a hotel, which I occasionally do . . ."

"Yes?"

"But I'm not at all sure that I will actually make these calls. I probably will—that is, I think I probably will—but at the same time there is a doubt in my mind." Wilson rubbed his hands together and examined them thoughtfully. "Part of me, you see, seems to recognize these calls as being very necessary and urgent, but there is another part of me which evidently regards the matter in a different light. That is, as being relatively inconsequential. I simply can't explain it any better than that."

Joliffe again nodded with understanding. "You aren't hungry, are you, Mr. Wilson?"

"Oh, no."

"If you are, I can send for something."

"Thank you, no." Wilson felt no particular inclination to do anything. "Do you want me to go on?"

"Please."

"Another thing occurs to me. This afternoon, by various rather remarkable means, I undertook to come, voluntarily, to your firm, to discuss a certain service which I understand you are ready to provide. Am I correct so far?"

"Yes."

"Well, I have the feeling that my attitude toward you now should be somewhat testy and demanding. I have experienced certain indignities. For instance, I was required to smear dust on my face. I suppose it's still there. Is it?"

"A trifle."

Wilson touched his cheeks doubtfully. "I'm afraid I've forgotten my point."

"You were saying you ought to be rather angry."

"Yes. But I'm not, you see. And that's not all. I had a remarkable dream, or what seemed to be a dream. In any case, I have the distinct impression that I have been subjected to a humiliation and obscene exposure, possibly under the influence of drugs, added to the various other unpleasant experiences of the afternoon, and although as I say, I should be very snappish with you on this score, I am not even curious about it."

Joliffe seemed satisfied. "Very good, Mr. Wilson. That's a first-rate description." He tapped his spectacles against his knee, ordering his thoughts. "Now we can begin with the questions from the beginning. Please answer carefully. Give no names or other specific details which might identify you beyond doubt, but try to sum up, briefly, your career, including educational background."

"All right. Um, I was born in—"

"No dates, please."

"—in Chicago. I was educated at an Eastern preparatory school, where I excelled in tennis, and at Harvard, where I helped manage the tennis team, having failed to become a member of it. Strange how that comes back to me. I suppose I went to classes and so forth, but all I remember is the little black valise in which I carried train tickets and cans of new balls when the team made trips. I used to give practice workouts to the singles champion, and once I nearly beat him."

"More succinct, Mr. Wilson, if you please."

"Of course. Well, I went to business school—graduate school, you know—and then I went into banking, which was still respectable in spite of Roosevelt, and I managed to marry a debutante from the very top drawer. Emily was quite a pretty girl then, but I had the suspicion that eventually she would grow fat, which proved to be the case—"

"I'm sorry, Mr. Wilson. You're going just a tiny bit afield from a career résumé."

"Oh. Well. Ah, as for banking. It's been my professional life, that's all. I don't suppose you want the names of the banks or my positions as of certain dates?"

"No."

"Well, that doesn't leave much. I've been in banking for twenty-six years, come next February, and while I've shown no extraordinary gifts for it, nevertheless I've done well in every sense. I'm earning a substantial salary, I've built a home and have a summer place, I own a boat and two cars, I've put my daughter through private schools and college, and on top of that, I have every reason to believe that in another few years, by the time I'm well along in my fifties, I will be president of my bank, which is a sizable one." He paused, uncertainly. "Is that enough?"

"Yes, unless you want to go on."

"I don't think I do. It doesn't interest me much right now, and I can't see how it would interest you. Why is such a résumé necessary, anyway?"

Joliffe moved slowly around the desk to the chair behind it and stood with his fingertips drumming lightly on the leather surface of the back. "It isn't necessary, but it's useful, as a reminder to our clients of the context of their problems."

"I'm not a client yet."

Joliffe responded only with a slight smile.

"As for reminding me of my problems," Wilson continued, "you may have a point there. I have this sensation of remoteness." As he spoke, however, he was aware that this sensation—actually, an absence of sensation—was showing signs of erosion. A tremor of anxiety was evident in his mid-section; he glanced down, as if expecting it to be registered visibly, like a spot of gravy on his shirt. "I'm not a client," he repeated.

Joliffe eased himself into the chair. "Tell me, Mr. Wilson, when did you first hear of our service?"

"A week ago. One night I got a call from a man who said he was Charley—"

"Avoid last names, please."

"Well, he gave this name, the name of my college roommate, a man I'd known all my life. One of my very best friends, in fact."

"But it wasn't really your friend on the phone?"

"I knew it couldn't have been."

"Why not?"

"Because Charley killed himself last year." Wilson glanced directly at Joliffe and cocked his head quizzically.

"Killed himself. Well," said Joliffe, impassively. "And what did this imposter tell you, then?"

"He started talking about college days, trying to prove he *was* Charley, although I kept threatening to hang up on him. He told me things that—shocked me."

"What kind of things?"

"Nothing, really. I mean, just little things from our college days. But they were things that only Charley would have known, you see. Not just one or two, but a dozen. And then some other things, too. For instance, once when Charley and I were young fellows and working for the same bank, we went out and got pretty tight, and on the way back, as a kind of joke, we talked about switching wives for the night—just a joke, you know—and then we thought it would be funny to announce this to the ladies, too, pretending to be serious. So we stopped at Charley's house first, to pull the gag on Sue, and damned if when we got there we didn't see some man sneaking out the rear door, and it wasn't a burglar, either . . . I mention this merely to illustrate my point. This voice on the phone told me things that only Charley could have told me."

"How about the voice?"

"Oh, it sounded like Charley, all right. But then, he had an ordinary kind of voice."

"Well, who was it, then?"

Wilson laughed softly. "Oh, it was Charley, I guess. He kept talking. Pretty soon I stopped saying I was going to hang up. I was a little frightened, I suppose. Charley had been a good friend, but I had gotten used to the idea he was dead—and then to have him come back suddenly, as a voice in my telephone receiver . . . it was a jolt, I can tell you."

"Yes, I can imagine. But how was he supposed to have killed himself? With a gun?"

"It was in all the papers. Quite a dramatic incident. He leaped into an active volcano."

Joliffe raised his eyebrows. "Remarkable."

"A hundred people saw it—from a distance. Naturally the body was not recovered."

"So it was Charley's ghost that telephoned you. Well, what did he say?"

"He told me about the services your firm offered, in a vague sort of way. He was very excited. He urged me to consider applying to you as a client. He said it would be . . . a rebirth." Wilson stared down thoughtfully at the carpet. It was a rich rust-brown. "A rebirth, that's what he called it, and Charley was not the kind of man to use hyperbole. He was a trust specialist, if that means anything to you. Well, he went on like this for quite a while, and I, you see, was in an extraordinary mental state, trying to grasp the fact of his existence, so that I suppose I was unusually receptive to his words. That is, I was attempting with all my strength to believe it was really Charley, and so what he said to me about your services seemed to drive right into my mind, as if all of my usual defenses and reservations against anything new and strange had been shattered . . ."

He shook his head in a puzzled way and looked at the window. It was growing late. The last great streak of sunset gleamed on the horizon.

"I was in a daze," he went on, quietly. "That's what it was. A state almost of hypnosis . . . I don't remember hanging up the receiver. I suppose I did. I just wandered through the foyer and into my study and sat down there in the first chair I came to, and Charley's words kept running in my mind, over and over again. Especially the word 'rebirth.' I thought in a confused way of how it would be if I myself were reborn, and I wondered if I would be a man and an infant at the same time, something innocent but also knowing . . . It's impossible to explain it clearly, but I was terribly moved. I think I wept for a while, all huddled up in that chair, and I fell asleep, so that when my wife finally found me—it was past midnight then—my confusion was all the greater, because although I distinctly remembered the telephone call, I wondered if it hadn't been a dream."

"Did you tell your wife about it?"

"Lord, no."

"What happened after that?"

"Well, the following night I had an unusual feeling, a premonition that everything was going to be repeated. That is, I knew that the telephone would ring, that I would answer it, and that it would be Charley's voice again . . . and that my sensation of shock would recur. You see, if an impossible thing happens once, well, it may be a dream or a hallucination or some misunderstanding, even; the kind of thing that . . . well, that couldn't happen twice. But I knew it would happen again. I was afraid it would and yet I wanted it to. I remembered something Charley had said the night before. He mentioned the business about the volcano, and joked about it a little, and then he said that he'd really jumped into a volcano . . ."

"Yes?"

"And—and he said it was beautiful there."

"Beautiful."

Wilson nodded. "A figure of speech. He referred to his sense of rebirth, as a result of your firm's services."

"Well, did he call again?"

"Yes. He gave me instructions this time. They were quite simple. He said that in a few days—he didn't know when, exactly—someone would give me a piece of paper with an address written on it, and that I would be expected there a little after twelve noon of that day."

"Is that all he said?"

"No. He said I was to use the name Wilson, and—that once I had begun the process, there would be no turning back. In the sense, I suppose, that the opportunity would not be offered a second time."

Joliffe said nothing.

"And he explained that it would mean just . . ." Wilson shrugged " . . . just walking away from everything. But he assured me that no one would be hurt by what I did, and that my affairs would be handled on a strict and fair basis, which I did find reassuring, in view of Charley's professional experience in trust management. I mean, a man of his standing could hardly be mistaken on such a point . . . Well, the whole idea now appeared to me to have a powerful logic. I didn't need to be persuaded, and Charley was very matter-of-fact this time, as if it were only a question of clearing up details in a transaction already agreed on. It was like—well, like talking with a travel agent about the exact itinerary of a vacation trip, and yet . . . Let me put it this way. Part of me was convinced that I would do precisely what Charley suggested, and that it was as germane to my future as, say, the promotion to senior vice president which I am due to obtain in a year or two; and at the same time, another part of me was incredulous, in a quiet way, that I should entertain any such notions for a moment. But still, the part that wanted to follow Charley seemed to be a little more in control."

"How do you mean?"

"Well, I'd been living as a matter of habit for so long that the routine had lost its force. Does that make any sense? The grooves had worn down, so to speak, and the slightest nudge was enough to send me off in a different direction, with all of the old instincts of habit still spinning away, like the wheels of a trolley that's jumped its tracks. Oh, I don't mean that just any sort of push would have been enough. For example, I'm sure that I wouldn't have suddenly run off to Philadelphia to spend a weekend with some blonde. No, my habits were able to foresee that kind of thing, I think, and I would have been proof against a specific temptation. But Charley's call—this was impossible to predict. There was no set of defenses against that."

"To put it another way, you were ready for such a call."

"Yes, I suppose so. Ready. That's the word. I was ready. Suppose I'd dreamed those calls. It wouldn't have made any difference. But they weren't dreams, of course. This morning, as I was walking the last block to the bank, right in the middle of the crowd, someone—a youngish man, I think—he came up beside me and he said, 'Mr. Wilson?' and he handed me the scrap of paper. Then he turned off to one side and I lost him. So I knew it was all real."

"Were you excited?"

"No, not in the least. I felt mildly anxious, and disturbed, not being sure just what I would ultimately do. My mind was divided, you see. I was being drawn in some peculiar way, but my habitual self acted as a kind of brake . . . perhaps pretending that it would permit the process to begin, simply as a means of humoring a wild impulse. And that's about the way I feel right now—divided. . . . Strange, I've never spoken to anyone this way before. Is that the effect of the drug you gave me?"

Joliffe switched on the desk lamp, for the room had darkened considerably. He glanced at his watch.

"You must be hungry, Mr. Wilson." He touched a button on the communications box. "We'll have a tray up here in a few minutes." He stood up and put his spectacles carefully into their case. "My own part is over, Mr. Wilson, but if you'll just make yourself at home here, some staff people will be in shortly to do the detailed processing."

"I haven't agreed to be a client."

Joliffe smiled. "But you're curious to see the rest of it, I should imagine. You've gone this far. Why not find out more, eh?" He drew a cigar from his pocket, clipped it with a tiny pair of scissors, and lighted it. "Just remember, Mr. Wilson," he continued, blowing out a perfect circle of smoke, "you're in the middle of a remarkable experience. You may have some doubts about it—most of our clients do, to be frank—but I would suspect that already it's had a definite cathartic value to you. Don't you feel better?"

"Yes, I suppose I do."

"Fine. That's really the essence of our function, you know. To make our clients feel better." Joliffe seemed so satisfied with the situation that Wilson felt it would be a discourtesy to protest any further at that point, although his sensations of anxiety were still mounting.

"So, just relax, sir," Joliffe went on, as he took his hat from the coat-tree. "The food will be up shortly, and then, by the time you finish, the staff people will be in to see you." He paused at the door. "Good luck, Mr. Wilson."

"Thank you."

After Joliffe left, Wilson remained seated on the couch, thinking of nothing in particular, and gazing passively at the window. It was fully dark now. The lights in the buildings outside formed a pattern which was in a constant process of change, for as some were switched off with the departure of the last office workers, others were turned on, presumably by janitors and scrubwomen, and all the tiny winking lights together seemed to be spread across the face of a single giant structure. Wilson found the sight quite interesting. He watched it for some time. Whenever a light appeared, he felt oddly cheered, thinking of the minute pulse of energy that it had drawn from the central electrical system, and each time one vanished, it vaguely depressed him, for he had come to imagine the lights almost as little living things, and himself as someone who for the moment had been empowered to observe their world, to rejoice in their radiance, and to sorrow when they were so abruptly extinguished. Thus he studied the night scene of the city as he might have watched, by the hour, a colony of ants under glass, or a beehive, or an aquarium containing miniature sea creatures, and while it occurred to him that he should instead be actively pondering his present situation, he felt no particular urgency to do so. His anxiety, steadily increasing, seemed to be centered not on himself but on the lights. Surely, he thought, they would not all be turned off. Surely some would survive through the night.

Someone entered the room: a servant with a tray.

"Your supper, sir."

"Ah . . . thank you, very much."

The servant set the tray on the desk, bowed slightly, and without another word withdrew.

Wilson got up at once. He was definitely agitated now. The lights no longer held his attention. Just as the sight of some commuter dashing desperately through a crowded station toward his train will awaken, in the minds of the unhurried men he jostles, momentary fears that they, too, may be late, so the brief appearance of the businesslike little servant evoked in Wilson an imitative reaction that brought all of his apprehensions bristling up. He, too, must set about his affairs. No more mooning. He gave the tray, with its covered dishes, a glance, but reached instead for the telephone. First he would call his wife, then Mr. Franks, and then—

But the line was dead. He jiggled the receiver angrily.

It was useless.

He stared around the room, but of course there was no other phone. His vexation brought with it the sensation that he was completely restored to his normal state of mind. The drug—surely that tea had been drugged—had worn off now, he decided, and he looked with great suspicion on the tray that the servant had placed down so innocently. He would certainly not make the same mistake twice!

Well, if the telephone would not work, he would set out to find one that would—and perhaps he would just walk out of the building and have done with it all. Briskly he snatched up his hat and strode to the door, conscious that he had, through some unaccountable lapse, slipped into a false and perhaps dangerous position, from which he must at once extricate himself.

He opened the door and set off along a hallway. On each side were doors leading to what were presumably subordinate offices, and far ahead, at the end, was the usual bank of elevators. Reasoning that if the central switchboard were closed, none of the telephones in the other offices would be usable, Wilson went all the way to the elevators and pressed the call button of each, on the assumption that at night only one of them would be in operation.

As he waited before the blank elevator doors, somewhat nervously smoothing his clothing and adjusting his Homburg, and hoping that the smudges on his face would not attract attention when he reached the street, he became aware of faint sounds of activity emanating from the offices along the corridor. He heard the intermittent mumble of voices, and a variety of indistinguishable noises that could be caused by the shuffling of papers, the scraping of chairs on the floors, the gliding of file drawers, and so forth. In itself, this evidence of business operation did not disturb him, although he realized that it was late for an entire staff to be at work, but he had become so impressed with the unorthodox character of Joliffe's company (actually, he assumed that Joliffe was not the head of the firm, but rather some officer in it, perhaps comparable to an account executive), that he was not at all certain what might happen next. Suppose they found him absent from Joliffe's office and rushed out to prevent him from leaving? That notion was not so foolish as it might seem, for men who would drug a client's tea might be capable of anything. At this point, he recalled what had seemed to take place after he had drunk the tea, and he flushed with irritation and embarrassment.

To dismiss the picture of his encounter with the woman, he glanced up sternly at the elevator floor indicators. Each, however, still rested at ground level. He pressed the buttons again, vigorously. One of the elevators would surely be available, he knew, for otherwise the late-working staff members would be unable to descend. Nevertheless, even after he had pushed the buttons a third time, there was no sign of movement on the indicators, and he determined that he would use the stairs, if necessary, although he supposed that he might be a good forty flights above the street. He walked over to the door marked "Exit" and tried it. It was either locked or so tightly jammed that he could not open it.

Without pausing for reflection, he went straight to the nearest office door, pushed it open, and marched inside. At once he was nonplussed, for where he had expected to find an office of moderate size, with perhaps a desk or two and a filing cabinet, he was confronted with an enormous room that ran almost the entire width of the building and was full of men busy at a variety of occupations. Some were at desks, reading newspapers or working at jigsaw puzzles; others were engaged in little hobbies, such as gluing together ship models, while still others sat at their ease in comfortable chairs, reading books or taking part in games of chess or cards.

It was a perplexing scene, too complicated for Wilson to comprehend fully at once. He moved forward, thinking that although these men seemed to fall into the category of clerks—for they wore the little tan cloth jackets traditionally assigned to clerks in certain old-fashioned firms—they were clearly not engaged in clerical work, but rather seemed to be merely passing the time unproductively, with their games and puzzles. Then, too, he saw that they were well-padded with flesh, instead of conforming to the usual dried-up and bony pattern of middle-aged clerks.

He chose the nearest man, who was studying a stamp album. As he approached, the man looked up reluctantly, and Wilson realized then that his entry had produced not the slightest ripple of interest among the occupants of the huge room.

"Excuse me," said Wilson firmly, "but I'm trying to find my way out of the building. The elevators don't seem to be running."

The man hesitated, as if debating how to respond; his manner was polite, and he attempted to gloss over his delay by rising slowly from the desk, clearing his throat, adjusting his cuffs, and briefly examining his fingernails.

"Not running?" he said, pursing his lips and frowning slightly. "That's odd. Um, perhaps the night operator was away for the moment. Do you think you might try again?"

"I was standing there for at least ten minutes," Wilson said. "Isn't there some way he can be notified?"

"I can try, if you like." The man went without haste to a table nearby which supported an interoffice communications box, and painstakingly studied its markings. "This may be the one," he said at length, and pressing one of the buttons, he spoke into the machine almost at once, without waiting for an inquiry: "I have a gentleman here who wishes to leave the building."

A metallic voice responded: "Yes. That would be Mr. Wilson. Would you ask him to return to Mr. Joliffe's office, please? Mr. Ruby is waiting there."

"All right."

The man returned to Wilson, and regarded him with a kind of ironic reserve. It was puzzling. Wilson thought of the dust smudges on his face. Perhaps the man had resolved not to risk the possible breach of etiquette that would be involved if he mentioned the smudges, even while foreseeing that they would prove embarrassing to Wilson. But the man seemed to be looking at him with more compassion than the matter of smudges would call for.

"Did you hear that, Mr. Wilson?" he asked mildly. "They want you down at the end of the hall again."

"Yes—well, all right. Thank you."

Wilson turned around. He was baffled once more. He did not feel able to make an outright protest, and at the same time he was more than a little worried about the fact that events seemed to conspire to keep him prisoner. As he reached the door, he cautiously turned for one last look about the room. For an instant, he had the impression that every pair of eyes was fixed on him, and that something extremely peculiar was on the verge of taking place—that, for example, all those tan-jacketed middle-aged clerks would burst into shouts of derision—but then he saw approximately what he had seen at first, a scene of quiet, domestic activity. He thought, also, that he detected a familiar face or two: the bald man who had been his guide earlier in the day, and the servant who had lately delivered his supper tray, but he could not be sure, and just as he turned around again to pass out into the hall, he wondered if he had not seen a face still more familiar than these, a face that had swiftly been lowered. Whose face? And had the face been familiar—or merely the eyes? He did not know, but that single glimpse of something that bordered tantalizingly on recognition was extremely distressing, and as he stood once more in the empty hall, he found that he was trembling. Courage, he told himself; be firm, be dignified, insist on your rights. He tried to recall some incident in his past where he had acted boldly in the face of some similar foreboding, but none came to mind, and his impotence was at that moment underscored by the opening of the door to Joliffe's office at the end of the corridor, revealing a man's figure. A hearty voice came bowling down at him:

"Ah, there, Mr. Wilson!"

Silently, Wilson trudged back toward the office, his hat in his hand.

Mr. Ruby, who greeted him, was a portly little man with large dark eyes and the habit of puffing out his cheeks before each remark, as though his thoughts swelled up inside and then, beyond containing, exploded into speech.

Introducing himself as an assistant general counsel of the firm, he politely motioned Wilson to a chair, seated himself at the desk, busily fingered the contents of his briefcase for a moment as his cheeks gradually distended, and then briskly inquired:

"Well, what shall it be, sir—death or disappearance?"

"I beg your pardon?"

"Of course, let me explain. It's partly a matter of cost, partly a matter of personal taste. Some clients are naturally sensitive on the question of death, and prefer the alternative, although my own opinion is strongly of the opposite. That is, assuming that cost is not a decisive factor, death has many advantages. For example, insurance is quickly paid, estate settlement is readily effected, trust arrangements are immediately operative, and then on the emotional side, a loving family is not subjected to the drawn-out hopes and worries involved in disappearance. Death is cut and dried and final, Mr. Wilson, as I'm sure a man of your experience will agree upon a few moments' reflection."

Wilson felt terribly tired and dispirited. He thought that if he made another attempt to leave the building and it were frustrated, he would despair absolutely and simply lie down to sleep until morning. Should he try? He could not decide.

"Naturally, you have some questions, sir," said Mr. Ruby, encouragingly. "I might add," he said, as Wilson showed no signs of reacting, "that Mr. Joliffe remarked that you were an unusually perceptive client. I'm sure that you will have some penetrating observations to make on the respective merits of the alternatives."

"I'm not a client," said Wilson, defensively.

"Precisely, sir. You have signed nothing. You are absolutely right to make such a distinction at this point. Excellently put, Mr. Wilson." The lawyer paused to permit his cheeks to inflate. "You are beginning, quite properly, from the most basic premise—you are not a client!"

Mr. Ruby's enthusiastic assent did not allay Wilson's alarm, but rather increased it. He felt, perhaps illogically, that as a client he might at least have some rights which the firm would be bound to respect, whereas merely as an ordinary visitor, he would have no status whatsoever, and so he resolved to leave this dangerous and complicated question for the time being, and to return to Mr. Ruby's specialty.

"Um, you mentioned the cost of death. Would you mind expanding on that?"

"Glad to," Mr. Ruby responded. He leafed through

his papers to be sure they were in order, in the course of which he provided himself with extra space by pushing the tray which held Wilson's untouched supper a bit to one side. "Let me start," the lawyer said, "by describing to you what we call our first-class death. This costs in the neighborhood of thirty thousand dollars." He absently reached over to the tray and lifted the silver dish that covered the plate. "Well, Mr. Wilson, this seems to be your supper. Won't you take it, sir? It's still nice and warm."

"No, thank you. I'm not hungry."

"Well, then, as you wish." Mr. Ruby did not replace the silver dish, and a pleasing aroma of fried chicken rose from the plate. "That chicken looks delicious," he remarked.

"I'm afraid I couldn't touch it."

"Of course. As I was saying, thirty thousand dollars. This may seem high, but you must remember that we have to provide a reasonably fresh cadaver, identifiable as being yourself, which naturally would require the most expert medical and dental adjustments. Are you quite certain you don't want that chicken?"

"Absolutely sure."

"Pity," said Mr. Ruby, sniffing the air. "Well, to return to the first-class death. In addition to the sources of expense I have mentioned, there is the problem that the circumstances of death must be reasonable and natural and above all, simple. Simplicity is costly, Mr. Wilson. Suppose the body is discovered in a hotel bedroom, and that death is the result, say, of a cerebral hemorrhage. You might not think this would be difficult." Mr. Ruby allowed himself an ironic chuckle. "Believe me, sir, it is fiendishly troublesome! The surgery bill for a cerebral hemorrhage alone would stagger you. I can assure you, Mr. Wilson, we make no profit on these cases! But at the same time, we can do it. We can guarantee a death of this kind. It will stand up to the most rigorous tests."

"Are there . . . other kinds?"

"Others? Oh, yes, there are two others." Mr. Ruby gazed again at the uncovered plate. "It's a shame to let this go to waste, Mr. Wilson. Would you mind if I—?"

"Not at all. Please do."

"Thank you." Mr. Ruby delicately lifted a chicken leg from the plate and inspected it. "Well," he went on, "a second-class death, for example. This would cost you about twenty thousand dollars. It is in the category of accidental death, you see." He bit into the chicken and chewed the meat with relish. "The cadaver is struck by an automobile or falls from a window. Naturally, the effect of violence reduces the complexity of the surgery, although surgery still is required. Excuse me." He paused to wipe his mouth with the napkin. "Delicious chicken, sir! . . . The chief disadvantage of the second-class death is that the violence is a source of distress to the family, although this is offset by the fact that the double indemnity feature of insurance is invoked."

"I see."

"Then we have death of the third class," added Mr. Ruby, speaking between mouthfuls. "I refer, of course, to suicide, which is in the price range of fifteen thousand. Here, surgery is reduced to a minimum, because for the monetary convenience of the client, we arrange for the obliteration of all or parts of the body." He paused to pick his teeth. "Ordinarily, this means that the head is blown apart by the blast of a shotgun inserted in the mouth. You can readily see that dental surgery would be an extravagance here."

"Yes."

"But then, of course, with suicide, you risk severe family distress, if only on religious grounds," continued Mr. Ruby, buttering a piece of cornbread. "I don't recommend it to you frankly." He popped the cornbread into his mouth. When he had swallowed it, he glanced inquiringly at Wilson. "Do you want me to review disappearance for you, sir?"

"I think not."

"Good. I was hoping you would choose death. For a man of your substance, cost ought not to be decisive. Shall we make it death of the first class, then, Mr. Wilson?"

"No—I mean, I can't be sure—"

"Of course, sir. You can't be expected to decide at once. Think it over," said Mr. Ruby, pressing a button on the communications box. "There's a good deal else to be done, Mr. Wilson, and you ought to give this matter some consideration in the meantime. If I do say so myself, sir, the question of death selection may be the most important decision of your life."

Apparently in response to Mr. Ruby's signal over

the communications box, two other gentlemen entered the room at this point and were introduced to Wilson as trust officers. He did not catch their names, for he was in an understandable state of confusion, nor was he particularly aware of their appearance, except to notice that one was tall and the other one short.

"These are the trust instruments, Mr. Wilson," said the tall one, as his partner handed Wilson a set of documents impressively festooned with ribbons, seals, and stamps. "And your revised will, drawn in accordance with the requirements of the trust, naturally, and all predated, of course, and, moreover, since these instruments are, in a literal sense, forged, we have taken the liberty, sir, of forging your signature on them as well, to save you the trouble. Your real name is used, I should add!" The trust officer tittered modestly at his joke. "We show them to you sir," he added, "so that you may approve them, as a matter of information, sir."

Wilson stared wonderingly at the documents.

"It's the standard mechanism, sir," the officer went on. "The trust provides for liberal settlements on your wife and child, effective at the time of your death, deriving from funds resultant from your conveyance and assignment to us, as your trustees, of your holdings and properties . . ."

Wilson found himself no longer able to hear the trust officer's words because of a curious buzzing in his ears. He tried to ignore it, but it became louder, and the more he strained his attention toward the opening and closing of the officer's mouth, hoping to guess at the words in that way, the more difficult it was to maintain his sense of equilibrium, for as the buzzing increased, so did certain extraordinary perception, which he ascribed to the fact that he had eaten virtually nothing all day, and had been subjected to a continuous series of shocks and frustrations. For example, the documents slipped from his fingers, but instead of flopping to the rug, they appeared to float in the air and to glitter there with unnatural brilliance, and then he heard, above the buzzing, what was evidently his own voice shouting: "I'm not a client! I don't want to buy death!" and he was dimly aware that the trust officers had gathered up their papers, and that Mr. Ruby, the lawyer, had begun punching the communications box. Finally, after what seemed a considerable interval in which someone assisted him to drink a cup of hot soup, he found himself, strangely enough, witnessing a moving picture projected on a portable screen which had been placed at the far end of the room.

The subject of the film, it developed, was himself. He was seen first strolling rather pompously along a street, obviously unaware of the hidden camera that was recording his movements. When had they done it, Wilson wondered. That very day? His portly figure was clothed in the grey suit, true enough, but that was not conclusive, and the street scene itself was slightly out of focus—but as he watched the screen further and saw his unsuspecting self proceeding blithely through an unidentifiable crowd, his apprehensions mounted sharply. Why had this film been taken . . . and why was it being shown to him now? Intuitively, he grasped the reason. Of course, there was but one possible answer—a splendidly logical one, and when the scene abruptly shifted, he was fully prepared for what then flashed before his eyes: the episode in the boudoir, where he clearly committed the most savage assault upon the defenseless woman.

The projection machine stopped. The lights of the office were switched on, and two men in clerk's jackets proceeded to pack up the equipment and to rearrange certain pieces of furniture which had been moved aside to make room for the screen. Wilson observed them silently. He was almost relieved that the purpose of his entanglement with the woman had been explained; otherwise, he seemed free of all emotion, as if the accumulation of distressing circumstances had finally plunged away into a void of their own weight, bearing with them his entire stock of feelings.

As the projection men departed, Wilson noted that neither Mr. Ruby nor the trust officers had remained in the room, and that he was now alone there with an elderly, rather feeble-looking man in a black suit, who was sitting on the couch a few feet away.

"So now it's blackmail," Wilson declared calmly.

The old man smiled. There was nothing sinister about the smile. He was, in fact, a very meek-looking old man, the kind who might well sit on a park bench every afternoon, telling stories to children and feeding crumbs to the birds. He had, moreover, none of the polish and efficiency of Joliffe and Ruby; his white hair was unkempt in a certain way, as if he had attempted in vain to manage it, and on his coat front were tobacco ash, lint, and shiny spots probably traceable to food stains.

"Do you want to talk to me?" the old man inquired, cautiously, but then before Wilson had had an opportunity to reply, he added, confidentially: "By the way, I have a message for you, from that friend of yours you mentioned to Mr. Joliffe."

"From Charley?"

"That's the name. Well, Charley wanted me to tell you," the old man continued, his face wrinkling up in the effort of recalling the exact words, "that when you jump into a volcano, it's bound to hurt a little at first." He gazed uncertainly at Wilson. "Does that mean something to you?"

"Yes, I think so."

"I hoped it would. Well," the old man said, fumbling a pipe from his pocket, "you said something about blackmail, Mr. Wilson."

"I didn't mean—"

"No, it's quite all right. I don't blame you. But it isn't blackmail, you know. It's just a kind of insurance, that's all. It's easier to go forward, isn't it, when you know that you can't go back?"

"Can't go back?"

"No, sir," the old man remarked sympathetically, "you can't go back. You realized that, didn't you? I mean, from the moment you hung up after Charley's first call? Of course you did. That's why you were so disturbed, because you knew you'd be facing a lot of unusual experiences, some of them unpleasant, and you knew you would need every ounce of courage in your system—"

"You're saying that I can never go back."

"Not to the bank, not to your family, not to anything you left."

"I see."

"Of course you see. And you see because, in your heart of hearts, you don't really want to go back. You want to go forward. Don't you? You want to be reborn. You *are* being reborn, my friend. Those hurts you feel, those are the pains of being reborn." The old man leaned forward as he spoke these words, inadvertently spilling tobacco from his pipe bowl over his trouser legs. Wilson was touched by his obvious sincerity, by his indifference to his appearance, and even more by the kindliness of his weathered old face.

"But you owe it to yourself, this rebirth," the old man said earnestly. "The pain will leave you soon, and life will begin again—a new life, a beautiful life. Another chance. And tell me honestly, my boy, will you be missed by those who are left behind? And will you miss them yourself?"

"I . . . don't know."

"Your good wife, my boy, is she still the heart and center of creation for you? And are you that for her?"

"We . . . get along."

"And your child, your daughter. What about her, son?"

"Well, we don't see too much of her, actually. She's recently gotten married and lives out West with her husband. He's a doctor."

The old man nodded with every phrase, and from time to time actually reached out and patted Wilson's knee, an action which so increased Wilson's feeling of rapport that he discovered that there were tears in his eyes. He did not brush them away.

"Excuse an old fool's prying, son," the old man said, "but what about the usual way of your life? I mean, did you look forward to your game of golf, for instance, or your staff meetings down at the bank?"

"You mean, do I like anything about the way I lived? Well, sir, I find that hard to answer. I was comfortable, I guess. I didn't think too much about things. I left my wife pretty much alone, and she did the same for me. We never quarreled, and in recent years we hardly ever—well, expressed much affection . . . and I did have my boat in the summer, and you're right, I did like to play a little weekend golf, and daub away with my watercolors sometimes in the garage . . ."

Wilson's voice trailed off. He clenched his fists, resisting an impulse to fling himself at the old man's knees and weep bitterly.

"So, this is what became of the dreams of youth," the old man remarked softly, as if he were simply musing aloud to himself. "Well, son, it's nothing to be ashamed of. You've done no worse than most men. You're a good boy at heart, and you've lived an honest life. It's just time to change, that's all." He gazed with affection at Wilson, who slowly bowed his head into his hands. "Now, son, I know what you're thinking. There's a tiny little thought still in your head, and that thought is summed up in one word: 'Desertion.' Well, don't you worry about that. You've taken care of the financial part of it, and as for the rest, well, you don't need them any more and they don't need you. They've got their problems, it's true, but you can't help them, just as they can't help you."

"I can see that now, sir," mumbled Wilson from between his fingers.

"What you need, son, is a good night's sleep. Then you'll be fresh in the morning, just like a baby. There'll be a few more details to clear up, but my boys will be working on them, don't you worry."

"Your boys?"

"That's right, son."

"Then you're the head of the company?"

"I'm afraid so, son. They usually call me in when there's what they call a difficult case. What they really mean, I think, is that there's a soul worth the saving. There never was a struggle in the soul of a good man that wasn't hard. Believe me, son, I know."

"I believe you."

"So you feel all right now, my boy?"

"Yes, sir."

"That's fine. Then we'll just pack off to bed, won't we?"

"Yes, sir."

CHAPTER 2

WILSON AWOKE in the morning to the familiar sound of an alarm clock, but even as he reached out to turn it off, he realized by the variation in pitch that it was not his own, and he sat up quickly, staring all around the strange room he was in, as if an analysis of his physical surroundings might lend some coherence to his disorganized recollections of the events of the previous day.

He seemed to be in a hotel bedroom. The top of the dresser was covered, in hotel fashion, by a sheet of glass, and his suit, hanging alone in the closet, had a forlorn and transient air. The pajamas he wore were new; he only dimly recalled having put them on, so exhausted had he been the night before when they had helped him to the room.

They. Yes, of course—they. He went to the adjoining bathroom, fully aware as he did so that he was not in a hotel at all, but still on the premises of the company whose client, it seemed, he had become, and as he inspected the sink and the cabinet, he was again reminded of the completeness of the services provided, for there was a full set of toilet articles awaiting his use, and furthermore, when he returned to the bedroom, he found that breakfast had been left for him on a tray, during his absence. There were two pills on a separate dish, with a note which bore the words, "For Mr. Wilson," but he did not take them.

As he ate, he wondered idly about his wife and about Mr. Franks, the senior vice president at the bank. Were they frantically telephoning one another by now? Were they in touch with the police? Or could it be that they had not missed him yet? This idea struck him ironically as being the most likely of all. Perhaps no one had particularly noticed his absence. Would he ever really be missed? Days might go by, even weeks, he mused, and then, quite by chance, his wife might decide to organize a dinner party for eight, say, and in the course of reviewing seating arrangements, would discover, to her annoyance, that he was simply nowhere to be found. He wrinkled his face, silently mouthing what he imagined would be her complaint: ". . . how troublesome it will be. He *knows* how hard it is to find an extra man to make up a party!"

As for the bank, well, that would be a different story, because the bank was more efficient. His absence would be readily noted, but he would not be missed as a person. No, the officers would stride around fretfully, asking whether anyone had seen the vice president in charge of industrial credit operations, who had unaccountably been mislaid.

In the midst of these reflections, which he indulged while recognizing them as a form of self-pity perhaps intended to conceal a real sense of worry and guilt, the door to his room swung open and a woman entered.

"Good morning, Mr. Wilson," she said briskly, as she advanced. "I hope you enjoyed your breakfast. You'll need it. You've got a busy schedule today." She seemed to be about his own age, but because she was smartly groomed and dressed, she looked no more than forty. "Oh," she remarked, eyeing his tray, "I see you forgot to take your pills. Well, you've still got your coffee left. You can swallow them down well enough with that, I should think . . ."

Wilson, meanwhile, had mumbled a confused and hasty response, and sat fidgeting in his chair, feeling at a great disadvantage for the want of a bathrobe, and not knowing whether to stand up and risk the parting of his unfamiliar pajamas, or to remain seated, which would border on a discourtesy. Was the woman a nurse or what? He could not be sure, but the genial note of authority in her voice, coupled with his own inferiority in attire, led him obediently to gulp down the pills.

"What are they for?" he asked meekly.

"For your nerves."

"I'm—not nervous, really."

"Well, in any case, it's standard procedure."

"But look here," he added suddenly, "I really ought to get some word to my wife—"

"Why?"

"Well . . ." He hesitated.

"Now, Mr. Wilson," his visitor declared, with a reproving smile, "you're supposed to put all of that sort of thing out of your mind. That's why you're here. You're paying *us* to take care of those details. Don't you fret about them. We've got them well in hand."

Again, Wilson felt humbled. Of course, the woman was right, he decided, but at the same time he was irked at the fact that he had been placed in such a vulnerable position—to be confronted without warning by a woman when he was not even properly dressed. It was deliberate, he thought. They wanted to keep him in a docile state of mind, by a combination of social unease and pills.

"You said something about a busy schedule," he said.

"Yes. First, you go to the Delivery Room."

"I beg your pardon?"

She smiled. "That's what we call it. The Delivery Room. You're being reborn, you know. Isn't it logical? Well, actually it's our surgery. Completely modern in every respect."

"Ah, yes. But—why surgery?"

"My, you *are* a little jumpy, aren't you?" She clucked, in mock disapproval. "Look here, you'd better slip into bed again and let me take your temperature, and then I'll tell you all about it." He glanced uneasily at the rumpled bed, and she added, with a hint of maternal solicitude, "Come on, now. You'll be much more comfortable there . . . That's it. Good."

She took a thermometer from a case inside her purse and put it in Wilson's mouth, gave the covers a professional touch to smooth them, and looked briefly at her wristwatch.

"Now," she said in a bright little voice, as if she were about to tell him a bedtime story, "in the first place, you've got to go to the Delivery Room to let the doctors get accurate measurements of your body, so they can pick the right size from Cadaver Storage. It wouldn't do to have one too tall or too short, you know. Well, and then they've got to make certain kinds of special casts of your teeth and your hands and so forth. It's all very complicated and scientific, but they do just marvelous work, and of course it doesn't hurt you the tiniest bit, but they need to do it, you understand, so they can process the cadaver to meet your specifications. You're having a first-class death, I think . . . Yes, I'm sure of it. Well, anyway, that's the first stage, and they don't want to waste time, because you're supposed to be found dead tonight."

Wilson sat up.

"The cadaver, of course," she added, gently poking his chest to make him lie down.

He remained sitting and took the thermometer from his mouth. "I understand that. But you said that's the first stage. Is there a second, then?"

"You're not worried, are you?"

"No, I just want to know."

"Aren't you feeling drowsy?"

"Not a bit. Would you mind telling me—"

"Well, all right. I must say you're a sensitive type, though, Mr. Wilson." She clucked at him again. "The second stage is cosmetic, naturally."

"I don't quite grasp—"

"Cosmetic. You can't go out into the world looking the way you do, you know. You'd be recognized at once."

Wilson sank back. "Of course," he muttered.

"Believe me, Mr. Wilson, you'll be amazed by what a little change here and there can do for a man. You'll feel younger—and you'll look younger, too. And that'll mean you'll *be* younger," she went on, soothing him with little pats on the forehead as he lay staring up at the ceiling. "Don't you want to be younger? Goodness, *I* wouldn't mind a little tinkering like that myself, one of these days. You can just thank your lucky stars you can afford all of this. Not that you aren't a fine-looking gentleman as it is, Mr. Wilson, but even the best of us can stand a weeny bit of improvement now and then . . ."

Her voice was gentle and chatty, but it did not completely set his mind at ease. It occurred to him that it had been confoundedly unfair of Charley not to have mentioned this right away. But then, why hadn't he thought of it himself before this? It was obvious enough.

"Look here," he said, interrupting the woman, "don't I get a chance to, um, approve the . . . the final version, beforehand?"

"Well, we used to do that, but we found that our clients could never really come to a decision. They kept adding a little here and wanting to take a wrinkle out there, and, really, it was a terrible nuisance, and so we dropped that feature."

"I'm not at all sure I like the idea."

"Mr. Wilson, we aren't going to have a little problem with you, are we now?" She shook her forefinger at him playfully, and Wilson was again impressed with the company's slyness in assigning a woman to deal with him. As a gentleman, he could hardly make a violent protest in her presence, and besides, the idea of being given a more youthful appearance somewhat intrigued him, especially since it had been urged on him by a woman who was by no means unattractive; which, he assumed further, was still another evidence of the craftiness of the company, in placing this phase of his processing in the hands of a female.

Nevertheless, his expression remained quite worried, and the woman regarded him anxiously.

"Don't you feel a little sleepy now?"

"No, I don't think so."

"You should, you know. From the pills. Goodness, Mr. Wilson," she said, placing her hands on her hips and frowning down at him, "we can't have you trundled off to Delivery all nervous like this."

"I'll be all right."

"We can't take any chances on that. After all, it's my responsibility. Well," she added, rising from the chair beside the bed and going toward the bathroom, "we'll just have to give you something more, to calm you down."

"Really—" Wilson began, but she had gone into

the bathroom and had closed the door behind her. He sighed, and feeling in reality somewhat drowsy, turned over on his side, facing the wall, closed his eyes and waited for sleep to come, wondering indolently whether he would awake to find that the plastic surgeons had already completed their work. Would he be permitted to glance in a mirror beforehand, for a last look at his old face?

But before he was quite asleep, he was aware that a pair of hands was quietly unbuttoning the jacket of his pajamas and, more remarkable still, was also pulling loose the drawstring of the trousers. In his somnolent condition, he half-imagined that he was a child, being changed in the middle of the night, and so he lazily wriggled, to help the unseen parental figure slip his pajamas off; then, when he lay naked, and felt the hands that had undressed him begin to knead his shoulders, he grew more wakeful, and decided that the woman was giving him a rubdown, to relax him physically while the pills became fully effective. However, the hands moved to his chest, then to his stomach, where they no longer rubbed but stroked and alternately scratched gently with slow upward motions of the fingernails, and then in a moment, to Wilson's considerable surprise, they descended still lower, where they commenced a delicate massage of a nature he doubted was prescribed in the pages of a nurse's manual. It was at this point that he turned over.

The room was dark, for the shades had been pulled and the curtains drawn.

"Is this supposed to calm me down?" he asked.

"Not at first. But it will later." Her voice still had its characteristic note of efficiency, despite the fact that she now was ministering to him on a far from impersonal basis, for she lay beside him, unclothed, with her unbound hair coiled down around her neck and shoulders.

"I frequently find this necessary with our more sensitive clients," she added, taking his hands and placing them against her breasts. "Not that I mind, really. I mean, it's part of the job, and someone who doesn't enjoy their work . . . well, they ought to do something else, don't you agree?"

"Certainly," said Wilson, somewhat thickly.

She kissed him. "Goodness," she remarked, her hand having explored his body once more, "you woke up fast, didn't you! Well, remember now, haste makes waste. Don't hurry. Kiss me all over." And as he complied with her request, she lay on her back, from time to time directing his mouth and hands with expert little movements, until after some minutes she provided him with final guidance, and they struggled harmoniously there, but only for a short time.

"I'm sorry," said Wilson.

"Not at all. I mean, it's not as if you did this every day, you know. You're not the kind of gentleman who goes running around after chorus girls, after all, and I would suspect that your wife has passed her peak years." She patted his shoulder reassuringly. "Tell me honestly, Mr. Wilson, when was the last time?"

"Oh . . . three months ago, or longer."

"There now. You see? When a man's out of practice, it just takes a few seconds, and then—zip!" She snapped her fingers. "All over and done with. But you've got nothing to be ashamed of, Mr. Wilson. Goodness, some gentlemen are impotent, and believe you me, I've really got my work cut out for me in those cases." She exhaled a little reminiscent sigh at the thought of these special labors. "Oh, but there aren't many of them, actually, mostly because our clients feel sort of at home with a person who's not exactly a child. They're more apt to be relaxed with a mature woman, don't you think? Someone who reminds them of their wives . . . That's the theory, anyway." She studied Wilson's face, "How do you feel, Mr. Wilson? Tell me. I'm really interested. As a person, I mean."

"I do feel relaxed," he answered, honestly. He was silent for a moment, pondering. "It's strange," he added, "but there's a kind of logic to it all. Let me put it this way. This morning, for example, certain remarkable things have happened to me, not the least of which was the act of adultery, to use a prudish term. Now, I'm not an adulterous man, really, but I feel no guilt at the moment nor do I think I ever will, simply because it all seems quite natural and simple, and—well, logical. I suppose it's partly because, as you have said, you are a wifely kind of person. And then yesterday, what happened then was logical and familiar, too, in a way. Granted that I was in a semi-drugged condition much of the time, still it amazes me, in retrospect, that

the whole process didn't strike me as being fantastic—
beyond belief. I *did* believe it, though, and that's why
I went through with it, barring an occasional objec-
tion, and I think the reason for this was that the whole
framework of the operation was businesslike and efficient. In short, I was confronted with a process that
was, perhaps superficially, quite familiar. The process
of providing guidance, advice, and services to a client,
roughly similar to the manner in which I myself have
been trained, with the exception, of course, that where
I have dealt with money, this company deals with
human beings."

"Oh, yes," the woman said, "the company's very
up to date. The whole idea is to treat the client as a
complete person and make him feel at home, whether
at work or play. Only, the difference is that we *care*. I
mean, our entire purpose is to serve the client. His happiness is all that's important to us. Really," she added,
waltzing her fingers playfully across his chest, "if we
don't succeed in providing that service, then we've
failed. That's what our president says, over and over."

"I'm sure that's right," Wilson said, remembering
the kind-faced old man who had conversed with him
so reassuringly the night before. "As a matter of fact,
that's supposed to be the guiding principle in banking
nowadays, too. We adopted a new motto a few years
ago, for instance. 'The Friendly Bank.'" He smiled
drowsily. "Of course, it didn't make any difference.
We didn't care any more about our clients, personally,
than before, but our public relations man made a very

strong case at the time for that motto. He said, as I recall, that people were terribly anxious to feel that they were wanted, and that if our corporate image—that was his phrase, not mine—if our corporate image could only wear a friendly smile, why then they would come flocking to us with their funds. Well, nothing happened. I suppose it was because we were still too strongly bound to the old tradition, thinking that people wanted us to handle their money, when they really wanted us to love them . . . Now," he added, from the depths of his sleepiness, "that's a strange thing for a banker to say."

"But you're right. That's the whole point—loving. *We* love you, Mr. Wilson. Yes we do." Her voice seemed inexpressibly soothing to him now, and with a sigh of gratitude, he turned toward her. "You just cuddle up and forget about everything," she went on, drawing his head down so that his face nestled into the warmth of her bosom, and clasping him close with a faint rocking motion of her arms. "Isn't that better now?"

"Mmmmm."

"You're going to sleep, aren't you?"

"Mmmmm."

"That's the boy. That's the good boy." She continued the rocking motion and at the same time began to hum softly what sounded like a little nursery tune, which sent a purr flowing from her body to his. He seemed to be sinking deliciously into a fragrant sea of tenderness, lulled by her faraway voice. "That's my goodykins. That's my sweet lamb . . ." The sea received him entirely.

It was warm, protective, and wholly his, and it caressed him sweetly with the vibrations of her lullaby.

He regained consciousness only once during the operation. He was lying on his stomach, his head turned to one side, and when his eyes opened, he beheld the naked body of a man occupying a similar position on an operating table some six feet distant. The face, turned his way, seemed familiar, and the longer he examined it, the more convinced he became that it was his own, but unpleasantly distorted, as if it were paralyzed in some fixity of emotion—laughter or fright, he could not tell which.

At any rate, Wilson assumed that he was seeing his own body, perhaps reflected in a mirror or possibly projected through some hallucination produced by drugs, and so he was concerned to see a man in white bend over the naked figure and begin to pluck delicately at the eyebrows with a pair of tweezers. Wilson waited for the prickings of pain; they did not come. He tried to move his hand up toward the eye, in vain, but when he sought to speak he produced a kind of grunt that encouraged him to try again. It was here that the man in white stopped his work, turned, and gave a peremptory signal. Someone clapped a rubber mask on Wilson's face, and he sank regretfully into oblivion once more.

When he at last awoke, he was in bed in what had every semblance of being a private room in a hospital. The walls were white. There was an odor of disinfectant. On the table beside the bed was a gay bouquet of flowers with a card bearing the words: "Warm personal regards—Charley." There was a transistor radio, too, softly tuned to symphonic music, and stacked beside it were several paperback mystery novels.

Wilson's face felt prickly. He reached up to touch it and saw that his fingers were wrapped in bandages; he thought that his face was bandaged, too, but because of his wrapped hands, could not be sure. Finally, he managed to work his pajama sleeve up above his wrist, so that he could press his face with the bare flesh there, and he was able to confirm his first impression. The entire lower part of his face was apparently bound by tape and gauze, and his jaws throbbed rather painfully. He moved his arms and legs in an exploratory way, and wriggled his toes; he was relieved to find that only his face and fingers seemed to have been involved in the operation.

A nurse appeared, all in white.

"Doctor is coming," she whispered reverently, and vanished.

Wilson continued to take inventory of his physical condition. He tried to speak, but could only croak dismally. His throat was sore, and he wondered if the surgeons had not fiddled with his vocal apparatus, too, to change his voice. Would his baritone now be bass or tenor? Or would it be higher than that . . . ? The disturbing thought crossed his mind that the company's medical men might have officiously made some permanent and radical alteration which, while it certainly would reduce the chances of his future identification, would never have received his prior approval. He wished that the nurse had addressed him by name. Would it be Mr. Wilson still, or Miss Wilson? He shuddered at the idea; but managed to gain some reassurance when he pressed his bandaged fingers around the area concerned, and felt no pain.

"Doctor is here," whispered the nurse, appearing once more.

The gentleman who entered the room was dressed not in a surgeon's smock but in a black suit, like a clergyman's. He was lean and grey, and his face bore the scars of some terrible accident, which gave him an impressive expression of spiritual agony.

"All right, Wilson, just lie quietly," he declared, somewhat brusquely, sitting beside the bed and staring at its occupant in a penetrating way. "You can't talk yet because we yanked all your teeth and you're sore all up and down, eh? So I'll do the talking." He seemed almost to enjoy Wilson's alarmed movement at the news about the teeth. "You'll feel better in a few days, though. Don't worry. And later on when you get a look at that new mug we're giving you you'll be prancing about like a stud bull, no doubt. Just be patient for a while, until we can get you ready for the world again."

The doctor at this point held up a folded newspaper before Wilson's eyes. It was opened to an interior page where the obituaries were carried; one of these items had been circled in red ink. Wilson saw that it was his own death notice, but before he could read more than the first few lines, the doctor took the paper away again.

"You were found very nicely dead of a stroke in a hotel," he said. "All quite ordinary and simple, just as you were told it would be. Funeral services tomorrow. And then you'll be cremated. Any questions?" He grinned rather wolfishly at Wilson. "Since you can't ask any, I'll have to guess them . . . As for your operation, we've begun grafting and ironing out, plus a chin-lift and earlobe trim, all of which will take about ten years off your appearance. We had to yank the teeth, you know, but you've got permanent choppers in place now, and in a week you won't know the difference . . . No, we didn't castrate you, Wilson. That's something every man seems to have on his mind . . . When I say 'we,' I speak editorially, of course. I'm the house physician, in permanent residence, not a surgeon, but your face was carved up by two of the best grafters in the business, and very high-priced, too."

Wilson was uneasily struck by the doctor's almost sarcastic manner of speech, and it occurred to him, too, that the man's scarred face was not the most eloquent testimony to the skill of plastic surgery.

The doctor seemed to divine his thought. "You're wondering if you won't turn out like this?" he asked, tapping one marked cheek. "Set your mind at rest, Wilson. It takes money to pay these flesh mechanics. You had the price. I didn't and don't quite yet. That's the simple answer . . ." He frowned moodily at his fingernails. "They keep promising me next month, but it's always next month, and somehow there's always a backlog of clients to be worked up first. Which is true enough . . ."

He sighed, then gave Wilson a sharp look. "You think you're the only one today? Not on your life, Wilson. There were eight of you shuttling in and out of surgery all during the night. Eight. Don't you believe me? Take a look at this . . ." He whipped open the newspaper again to the obituary page. "Fifteen gents are listed here, each one rich enough to warrant a few paragraphs, and eight of 'em are right here in this building now, alive and kicking under bandages, like yourself . . . One cheapskate bought suicide, and—let's see—three others went out second-class, and the rest, you included, took cerebrals . . . Eight in one day. And that's nothing. Sometimes we handle ten or twelve, especially in the dog-days in late summer, when everybody's depressed and wanting a change. Can you imagine what that means, Wilson? Something like three thousand guys produced every year right on our tables. If I had a buck for every hunk of meat and skin chopped off there, I'd be a rich man . . . All I know is, I'd hate to be in the Cadaver Procurement Section in the busy season. If business expands any more, they'll have to start making 'em out of plastic to fill their orders. We've got a research department working on some of these problems. For example, how long can you keep a stiff in cold storage and still fool the medical examiners? That kind of thing . . . Pigmentation, too. We can get plenty of bodies from Latin America, but most of 'em are on the short side, and then the skin tends to be darkish. You can mess around with features all you like, but you can't just slap on a coat of white paint and expect the survivors to be happy, can you? Well, we'll solve that one, too, in time. As it is, we're using the Latins for a lot of our second-class jobs, where details aren't so important ... Even so, Wilson, there are some slip-ups now and then. We're only human. Last week, for instance, there was a big stink. This client said he wanted a real professional piece of work, which was understandable because he was ugly as sin. Well, as it turned out, the mechanics had some trouble with his nose, or maybe his jaw. They got off pattern somehow, but they figured he looked pretty good anyway, and so they finished the job and packed him off to his beautiful new life—with him looking like the image of Franklin Roosevelt. Not bad, huh? Except this moneybags happened to have been honorary Republican state finance chairman somewhere at one time. Boy, did he raise hell when he saw a mirror! But there was nothing they could do about it, so this rich bastard is out in the world today, I guess, a walking reminder of the good old New Deal ... There's a kind of poetic justice in that, Wilson, don't you think so? ... Wilson? Well, I see you're asleep again ... Guess I shook you up a little, didn't I? They handed you all that crap about love and rebirth, and now you find out it's just a butcher shop, like everything else, so you don't want to hear about it ..."

For the next several days Wilson remained in a state of lassitude, unvisited except by the nurse, who tended to his physical needs, and by the doctor, who occasionally appeared to poke the various bandaged areas, and to ask, "This hurt much?" Each time, the pain was less, and Wilson's voice returned gradually, too, which he found convenient, since hitherto he had been unable to communicate his wants except by signs, inasmuch as his wrapped fingers were unable to hold a pencil for writing.

On the fourth day, a little bushy-haired man entered, lugging what seemed to be a small square suitcase, which he opened on the floor, out of Wilson's line of sight, and tinkered with for a few moments.

"Excuse me, sir," the little man said finally, straightening up and drawing a chair close to the bed. "My name is Davalo. I'm your guidance adviser." He smiled in a self-deprecatory way at the use of the title. "I have reference to your future career."

"I'm afraid I haven't thought much about that," said Wilson, truthfully.

"Pardon me, but you have, sir."

"I'm sorry . . . ?"

"Permit me, please." Mr. Davalo stooped toward the hidden suitcase. There was a sharp click, followed by a gentle whirring sound like that of a recording machine, which Wilson deduced it was when he heard his own voice issuing from its general direction:

"I want a big ball, a big red ball," Wilson's voice chanted solemnly. "A big big ball, a red one . . . ."

Mr. Davalo plunged at the machine. "I'm sorry," he muttered, grunting with the effort of bending. "I'm afraid we picked you up a bit too early." He cleared his throat in an embarrassed way. "We recorded this while you were under gas, you see, and there's always a touch of infantilism to begin with, but later"—he stood up, slightly flushed—"we develop a more mature expressional infrastructure . . . and if you'll bear with me, sir, I believe I have located it now."

Once more Mr. Davalo turned on the recording machine. His own voice was the first to be heard. In a wheedling tone, it inquired:

"What would you like to do most of all? Most of anything in the whole world? Hmmm?"

"Most of anything?" responded Wilson's voice.

"Of anything."

"Well, um. I'd like to be a tennis king, like Bill Tilden. That's what I'd like most."

"Yes, I see. Well, and what after that?"

"That's all."

"Ahem. Well, suppose you couldn't be a tennis king, for some reason. You'd have to do something else, wouldn't you? Of course. Well, you think about it, and you tell me what that something else would be."

There was a considerable pause following this question, during which Mr. Davalo waited with a small and confident smile. Then Wilson's voice was heard again:

"Oh, I guess . . . well, I guess I'd like to paint stuff. I mean, like mixing up colors and painting things, you know."

"Pictures?"

"Pictures and things. Chairs and walls, too. And coloring in magazines. Not old magazines, but new ones, before anybody gets to read them. And especially walls. I don't know just why, but I get this sort of urge to put things on walls, you know—"

"Well," interrupted Mr. Davalo briskly, turning off the machine. "No need to listen to any more, sir. I think the creative wish-pattern there is pretty self-evident, and without going into any of the technical assumptions underlying my analysis, I should think you'd agree that—to put it in plain, unvarnished English, Mr. Wilson—that your obsessive motivations strongly indicate artistic pursuits as being basically responsive to your particular development as an integrated human being."

"You mean I ought to be a painter?"

"Yes."

"And you say all of this was recorded while I was under gas?"

"During your adjustment, yes, sir. The particular portion I replayed for you was at psychological age fourteen, Mr. Wilson, which we find the most revealing, for there is sufficient articulation by then and at the same time little of the superimposition of adult goals which one encounters by, say, age sixteen."

"Well," said Wilson, dubiously, "it sounded to me more like my real desire was to play tennis. This business about painting seemed pretty tenuous—"

"Trust us, Mr. Wilson. We are trained to probe deeply, and to interpret. As a fourteen-year-old, you spoke haltingly, true enough, but to a specialist, your meaning was crystal clear."

"Are you a psychologist?"

"No, sir. Education is my area." Mr. Davalo colored with what Wilson assumed was pride. "Well," he went on, taking a set of papers from his pocket, "let's take a look at the program we have worked out for you, shall we?"

However, in the course of settling himself down in his chair, he inadvertently gave the machine a kick, and Wilson's recorded voice continued, ruminatively:

"—like once I was horsing around a barn up near Tarrytown with this girl Mary, see, and we got to throwing these cow-pies up against the walls with pitchforks, just as a gag. Don't ask me why—"

Mr. Davalo bent quickly to turn the machine off again, but his papers tumbled from his lap, and he chose to retrieve them first.

"—but anyway we did it," Wilson's voice droned on, "and it was a hell of a lot of fun, if you'll excuse the expression. Well, the funny thing was that it was sort of exciting, in a way. I mean—well, I can't quite explain it, but pretty soon this girl Mary kind of ran inside the barn and I went after her and she let me catch her on this pile of hay or straw or whatever it was, and darned if she didn't flop right down on her back, with her dress hiked up, and started—"

To Wilson's disappointment, Mr. Davalo cut off the

narrative here, and in a rather flustered state began reordering his handful of documents. Wilson tried to remember what had happened in that barn near Tarry-town, but he could recall nothing, and so was left in frustration. If Mr. Davalo were not such an old maid, he thought, he would ask him to play the rest of the recording later on.

"Getting back to painting, Mr. Davalo," he said, "I'm not sure that would be exactly right for me. I've been a Sunday painter of sorts, it's true, but I'm not much good at it, and I'm afraid—"

"Ah, but it's all arranged, Mr. Wilson. Here." Mr. Davalo began handing him the papers. "Your diploma in fine arts, sir, and your certificate of study abroad, including letters from the masters you worked under, plus notices of your first six one-man shows, and then here's a little portfolio of color photographs of some of your work." Wilson found himself fairly deluged with the papers, which with his bandaged fingers he could handle only with extreme difficulty. "You are an expert portraitist, Mr. Wilson," Mr. Davalo added, "and I'm glad to see you're in fine command of anat-omy and detail, sir. If I may say so, your pictures have a haunting quality about them. Realism in treatment, sir, but poetic imagery in choice of subject. Not that I pretend to be a critic of painting . . ."

Wilson glanced hastily at the documents, feeling that again questions of extreme personal importance had been settled far too speedily, without his approval.

"But these diplomas are from reputable universities," he exclaimed. "Surely such things could not safely be forged."

"That's not my department, Mr. Wilson, but I can assure you that every item is bona fide and valid. We've never had a single spot of trouble from that quarter, sir."

"But these paintings. How could I pretend—"

"You will be supplied with fresh paintings periodically, sir, while you perfect your own style at your leisure."

"But, good Lord, I could never approach a professional level, Mr. Davalo."

"Come, come, sir. Don't be so sure. In any case, you are already established as a painter, and with the income provided for in your financial arrangement, your living expenses will be met regularly." Mr. Davalo smiled patiently. "You are relieved of economic necessity, Mr. Wilson. You occupy a position of some dignity—nothing conspicuous, mind you, just the solid and mildly successful kind of thing. And you are free of any nagging considerations for others. See here, on the pamphlet that lists the works in one of your shows. You are a bachelor, according to this; the only son of deceased parents, and so forth. In short, you are alone in the world, Mr. Wilson, absolved of all responsibility except to your own interests and desires. Isn't it marvelous, sir?"

"I suppose so." Wilson pawed anxiously through the documents. "Wait a minute. It gives my first name her. 'Antiochus.' That's a terrible name to give a man, Mr. Davalo. Really, I must draw the line at that."

"I'm sorry, Mr. Wilson, but all of your records have been made up now."

"But it's a preposterous name."

"You'll get accustomed to it, sir. To my mind, it has a noble ring—Antiochus. Antiochus Wilson . . . a jewel of a name, if I may venture to say so. And besides, you are at liberty to use the diminutive 'Tony' if you like, in daily affairs. Take my own case. My name is Federico—a splendid name, but too elevated for ordinary purposes, and so I am known to my friends simply as Fred. In any event, sir, a man's name is a minor matter, don't you think? The man himself and his works—these are the important things."

"Somehow that sentiment seems inapplicable in my case, Mr. Davalo."

"Perhaps." Mr. Davalo began to close up the recording machine. "If you like, I can ask a member of the Documents Division to come in and explain the necessity for the name, sir. They do have their reasons, I'm sure."

"No, thank you. That won't be necessary. Um, could you tell me where Antiochus Wilson produces his paintings?"

"Your studio, sir? I believe it's in California somewhere. You'll find it all in the documents, which I will leave so that you may examine them at your leisure." Mr. Davalo lifted the recording case and inclined his head. "It's been a pleasure, Mr. Wilson."

"No less for me, Mr. Davalo," said Wilson, not without a touch of irony.

After his guest had departed, he raised the documents in his clumsy hands and stared at them for a moment. Then, with a sigh, he let them drop and lay solemnly against his bedchair, gazing for a long time at the blankness of the white wall opposite.

CHAPTER 3

THE PLANE rushed forward. Wilson braced himself against the motion, and grasped the arms of his seat. Outside, the dunes of snow along the runway fled backward, then dropped down and tilted out of sight as the plane began its climbing turn and headed toward the sun.

The aisle seat beside him was empty. He was thankful for that. "You'll be self-conscious at first," they had told him. "Don't worry. It's natural. It'll wear off in a day or two." They had been right this far. In the airport, he had felt that every pair of eyes had been turned on him, so that finally he had gone into the bar for a drink to steady his nerves. Now at least he would have a certain privacy for a few hours. Somewhat stealthily, he drew a pocket mirror from his coat and, for the hundredth time that day, examined his face.

The surgeons had done an extraordinary job. They had taken a face that tended to be rounded, florid, and a bit jowly, and had somehow made it lean and long and hard, with prominent cheekbones and chin; and the weeks and weeks of dieting and exercise that had accompanied the surgical process had produced a physique to match.

Only the eyes were the same. That morning when he had awakened in the airport motel and had gone cautiously over to the mirror, they had stared out of the strange new face like two old friends, bewildered and reproachful. It had been his first opportunity to examine himself, for although the last bandages had been removed two weeks before, he had not been permitted the use of a mirror.

"Would you like coffee, sir?"

"Oh. Yes, thank you, I believe I would."

Even the impersonal attention of the stewardess unnerved him. He wondered if she had caught him studying his mirror; tucking it away again, he picked up the newspaper he had purchased in the terminal, and sought to concentrate on the political columns of the editorial page. But his eyes strayed over to where the obituaries were carried, and he found himself reading each one suspiciously.

"Here you are, sir."

"Eh? Oh, thank you."

"Luncheon will be served in about an hour, sir. I hope you have an enjoyable trip."

"Thank you very much . . ."

The coffee tasted strong and rich. He sipped it gratefully, for it seemed to burn off the lingering fogginess in his head that was, he assumed, the legacy of the drug administrated the night before. They had handled him with their usual efficiency, for he had not the slightest recollection of what had happened. He had gone to bed, feeling remarkably drowsy, and then had awakened in the airport motel. What had occurred in between— how they had managed to transport him from their building all the way through the city and out to the airport—was a mystery. He had found himself attired in grey silk pajamas; on the luggage stand was a suitcase full of clothes, neatly packed; in the closet was the suit he now wore, and a topcoat and hat, and on the dresser, in front of the mirror where he would be certain to see it, was an envelope containing his airplane ticket and a typewritten note instructing him not to miss his flight, and, almost as an afterthought, providing him with his home address.

He was alone. Free. Different.

The pocket mirror was in his hand again; staring insolently out of it was Antiochus Wilson, a wolfish stranger who had gobbled up that plump banker and stolen his eyes.

He could not bear to look at it for long. To occupy his hands, he unwrapped a cigar and busied himself with the process of trimming and lighting it. It wasn't a bad face, he consoled himself. Far better than his old one, actually. It was just—well, it was just not his, that was all.

To his alarm, he saw that the stewardess was approaching with a fixed smile.

"I'm sorry, sir." She bent over him, her teeth gleaming. "Cigarette smoking only, I'm afraid."

"Oh, of course. I'm sorry." He stubbed out the cigar.

Possibly to soften the effect of her official reproof, she remained hovering beside him. "Haven't you been a passenger of mine before, on this flight?"

"Oh, no."

The abruptness of his answer seemed at odds with the routine requirements of the situation, however, and so he added, hastily: "I mean, maybe I have, but I'm not sure. I fly a good deal coast to coast, you see," he went on, feeling that he was struggling clumsily into contradictions, like a child spinning its first fib. "I'm a painter." Another idiotic remark. He hastened to explain it. "Well, not that a painter does a lot of flying, ordinarily, but I've got shows in galleries in the East, you see . . ."

He simply did not know how to get rid of her, or how to curb his tongue, and he thought he might have gone on chatting away indefinitely had not the sound of retching a few seats ahead drawn the stewardess to her duties.

Rebirth! Wilson hunched down in his seat. He would have to do better than this, he decided. He must get himself in hand. He could hardly enjoy his hard-won independence if he was going to be upset by the sight of his own face and the most ordinary demands of social intercourse with strangers. Whatever the drawbacks of his former life had been, he had achieved a certain self-possession in the course of it, and it was most distressing to find that resource missing, even temporarily.

Yes, he had had composure then, and . . . But he could not think of any other outstanding personal quality that he had possessed, and as a matter of fact, for some reason his past now seemed terribly remote, as if it had been the life of some undistinguished person he had read about idly in a book a month ago, and mostly forgotten. Even his experiences at the company were not vivid in his mind. As he lay restlessly back in his seat, the features and personalities of Mr. Joliffe, Mr. Ruby, and the rest resisted his efforts at detailed recollection. Things were jumbled. That enormous room full of middle-aged clerks . . . had he seen a familiar face there—or was he confusing this with some incident earlier on that first day, before he had gone out on his fateful lunch hour?

And his own face, his old face—would he forget that, too? He took his wallet from his pocket, and was opening it to take out the photograph of himself and his wife which had been taken three years earlier, during a summer on the Cape, before he realized that the wallet was a new one, and that, naturally, the company would have placed his old one in the clothing of the cadaver that had been found in the hotel room.

This wallet contained no pictures; only money, and a few identification and credit cards. He examined one of the latter. According to its date, it had been issued to Mr. Antiochus Wilson four years ago and was appropriately worn around the edges. He marveled at this additional testimony to the artistry of the company's Documents Division. It was amazing. Everything, it seemed, had been thought of; happiness, too, would surely be provided.

Shortly after his plane landed, Wilson was subjected to an experience which destroyed the degree of serenity he had attained during the last portion of his flight.

After having entered the airport terminal and claimed his suitcase, he consulted a map, which indicated that his studio-residence was within thirty miles of the city; he thereupon decided that he might justifiably make the trip by taxicab, as he seemed to have plenty of money, and he was starting for the main entrance to find the cabstand when he was hailed from behind.

"Tony! Tony Wilson!"

Alarmed, he hurried on. Again the voice called out; he lengthened his stride. The voice was pursuing him—no doubt of that. It was baying his name, gaining on him. Near the entranceway he paused, confused by the sudden sunlight, and when he felt the handclap on his shoulder, he gave up and slowly turned around.

"Tony—you old rascal!"

He confronted a large red-faced man dressed in Texan style with low leather boots and a ten-gallon hat, who seized his hand and pumped it vigorously.

"Good to see you back, Tony! Damned good! If I didn't have to make my plane, I'd make you buy me a drink right now, by God!" The man gave Wilson's hand a final wrench, punched him good-humoredly on the shoulder, and glanced at his wristwatch. "Nope—I just ain't got the time, Tony!" He backed off a few paces, still shaking with geniality, raised one meaty hand in a mock salute, and cried: "You be good, now, and leave them girl models alone, hey?" Then he turned and plowed away toward the bank of ticket counters.

Wilson went outside and with a trembling arm signaled for a taxi. The implications of the large man's greeting were too alarming to bear examination. He tried to ignore them, but they pressed up insistently into his mind all during his ride. He was further disheartened when he thought of returning to the airport and flying to some other city, for it occurred to him that he would be powerless to do so. He had no resources except the cash in his wallet. He had no notion of how to get in touch with the company back East, either, and even if he could, he was not at the moment certain that his financial arrangement permitted him to draw on his funds at will. He wiped his palms with his handkerchief, patted his clammy forehead, and stared out at the sun-swept countryside, gay with flowering shrubs and shaggy, comical palm trees.

Surely he had been the victim of a ridiculous coincidence. There must be a thousand Tony Wilsons in California. Ten thousand, possibly. And yet that beefy creature had spoken of models—girl models, which implied painting, surely—and how many of these Tony Wilsons would not only bear some resemblance to him but also be painters? He took a deep gulp of air. How many? It didn't matter. There would be at least one other—there *must* be, for the overriding reason that Antiochus Wilson had not come into public existence—literally and physically—until that very morning. Thus, there could be no ambiguity.

Nevertheless, his apprehensions refused to be quieted by such reflections, and he was still decidedly shaky when the taxi arrived at its destination. He got out, paid the driver, overtipped him, lifted his suitcase, put it down again, fumbled for his handkerchief, squared his shoulders, let them slump back, turned anxiously to watch the departing cab swing back onto the highway, and stood fidgeting in the driveway for some moments before he was able to muster the courage to approach the house.

Under different circumstances, he would have found the place most attractive. It was a modest ranch-style structure, with a portion of its roof made of glass, indicating a studio beneath, and it sat on a gentle rise that overlooked the ocean, which lay at some distance. Here and there were other homes, but none was close, and altogether it was a comfortable prospect that implied an income which would of necessity also be comfortable.

He approached the house warily, watching the windows for faces, wondering with every step if something unexpected and unpleasant would not come rushing out at him. All was quiet, however, as if the place were vacant, but still he quivered uneasily as he stood on the doormat, feeling in his pocket for a key he did not have. Finally he reached tentatively for the doorknob, but before he touched it, the door was swung open by someone inside.

"Welcome home, Mr. Wilson."

The speaker was a slight man with a grave expression on his face; he was dressed in a suit dark enough to be black, and in fact, with his air of somber alertness, he resembled a mortician's assistant maintaining a discreet composure for the sake of the bereaved, while at the same time covertly sniffing for the taint of physical corruption.

He took Wilson's bag and ushered him inside.

"I trust that your trip was not too fatiguing, sir."

"Um, yes. I mean, no, thank you." Wilson entered the living room furtively, still expecting something frightful to spring out at him from behind the chairs and sofas, or to rise from the conversation pit where, it seemed, a small fountain was bubbling.

"My name is John, sir," continued the black-suited man, politely. "I am assigned to you, sir, to help you through your initial period of adjustment." He cleared his throat with an air of modesty. "Not that you will require much assistance, Mr. Wilson, but there will undoubtedly be various questions in your mind which I will be able to clear up—to the extent of my authority, sir."

Wilson stared at the little man, who seemed obviously to be cast in the role of a personal servant.

"I think," he said slowly, "I'd like to wash up and have a drink—John."

The little man bowed slightly. "Very good, Mr. Wilson. Your room is right this way, sir. I've laid out a change of clothing for you on your bed, if you care to refresh yourself, and then perhaps when you've had your drink, I can satisfy any points on which you may be curious, sir."

Reassured by the man's manner of deference and competence, Wilson proceeded more composedly to his room, content for the moment to postpone all questions until he had quite recovered from his state of agitation. But already he felt much better, and his spirits were further lightened by the sight of his bedroom, which was large and tastefully furnished, and whose windows commanded a good view of the countryside and the ocean beyond. By the time he had taken a shower and changed into the slacks and jacket which John had laid on the bed, he was actually whistling and examining himself with a touch of pride in a full-length mirror. Not a bad-looking fellow, Antiochus Wilson. Lean as a leopard, and with the stamp of real character in that rugged, masculine face, which, the longer he studied it, seemed to suggest that here was a man who might have performed feats of courage and daring—as a soldier of fortune, perhaps—and who, if bronzed by the California sun and attired in evening clothes, could be considered downright handsome. In this more confident frame of mind, he left the room and made a brief inspection of the house.

The studio, which adjoined his bedroom, was appropriately furnished with unfinished paintings, which were hung on the walls, or stacked in corners, and empty frames, blank canvases, and jars of paints, all casually arranged in a condition neither disorderly nor artificially precise. In the center of the room was a large easel where a charcoal sketch of a nude woman was tacked, and propped at the base of the easel was a little watercolor of ocean surf breaking wildly against some rocks. Wilson was somewhat comforted by these last two items, for they were more amateurish than the other works displayed, and he thought, too, that with some practice he might do as well himself; indeed, it occurred to him that possibly the sketch and the water-color had been so prominently placed specifically for his encouragement.

The living room, where John was mixing a small pitcher of Martinis, was dominated by two walls of glass transparent only to those standing inside; a huge fire-place was squared off on a third wall, and directly across from it, beyond the conversation pit, were hung several paintings of rather eerie landscapes, which carried the initials "A.W." in one corner. A door near the fireplace opened into what Wilson assumed was the domain of his servant—a pantry, kitchen, and tiny bedroom—to which he gave only cursory attention before he returned to accept the drink John had prepared, and eased himself into a chair before the fireplace.

"I had a curious experience at the airport, John," he remarked at length, deciding to proceed with the interrogation of his servant, but in a circuitous manner.

"What was that, sir?"

"I was accosted by a large man dressed somewhat like a Texan. He seemed to know me; that is, he called me by name, although I was fairly certain I'd never met him." Wilson glanced questioningly at his servant who, however, remained impassive. "I suppose it was a mistake on his part," he added. "Don't you imagine so, John?"

"So it would seem, sir."

Wilson was not completely satisfied with this response, but resolved to abandon the subject for matters of more immediate concern.

"Tell me, John, are you familiar with the state of my finances?"

"Your accounts, sir? Yes, of course. Let me get the books for you."

Here Wilson's inquiry was more successful, for John produced a set of bank statements which indicated a checking balance that had lately been reinforced by a handsome deposit. John intimated that similar ample sums would be forthcoming every six weeks. Wilson was relieved to find that the company's pension was so generous, for in the confusion attendant on his sojourn at the company's headquarters, he had neglected to assure himself specifically on this point. It was a most efficient arrangement, and moreover, he learned that he was freed from the details of managing his new household, for it seemed that John was taking care of all routine expenses by means of a separate account established along the lines of a modest budget.

However, in the course of their discussion, Wilson

was struck by the fact that his servant never openly mentioned the company, nor even once referred to anything that would indicate that Antiochus Wilson was other than what he appeared to be: a well-to-do bachelor in his late thirties who pursued a moderately successful artistic career. The company's pension payments, for example, John guardedly identified as "proceeds of stock investments," and as for the supply of new paintings which Wilson would need to maintain his standing as an artist, John merely noted that these were to be received by post every two months, without suggesting that anyone except Wilson himself had actually produced them.

Wilson, relaxed by the effects of his drink, became ironically amused by John's evident desire to preserve the fiction of his new identity, but at the same time he judged that it would be imprudent for him to ignore it himself. In the first place, he *was* Antiochus Wilson, after all, and he should discipline his own mind to accept the fact, and then, further, he felt a certain reluctance to place himself on an intimate footing with a servant by initiating a discussion of personal matters. Nevertheless, he could not help speculating as to what an open and frank discussion would reveal, particularly about John, this sober little man who would, apparently, remain a part of his new life for quite a while. Presumably John had been trained by the company and dispatched to California to rent the house and make all of the other preliminary arrangements. And undoubtedly there were many just like him, schooled to act more or less as Sancho Panzas to the other quixotic gentlemen being reborn in such numbers on the surgical tables of the company. Wilson wondered whether John would stay with him merely long enough to see him properly launched, and then, being replaced by an ordinary valet, leave on reassignment to serve some more recently reborn client. In any event, Wilson decided, John's calling was a unique specialization even in a remarkably complex modern world.

He accepted the remaining contents of the Martini pitcher, and as he sipped from his glass, he became positively genial. His servant impressed him as being a fine, clever fellow, and his present situation was beginning to take on a most appealing aspect. He gazed with approval through the glass wall, which disclosed the grand sweep of countryside and thin blue strip of ocean.

"What kind of people live around here, John?" he asked at length.

"Professional people, sir, and some in business, and there are some who write, I believe."

"No artists, I hope," said Wilson, with a mock conspiratorial wink at his servant, but John treated the question with his customary gravity.

"I think you are the only one, Mr. Wilson," he said, and then, after a pause, he added: "Perhaps you'd like to give a small cocktail party for the immediate neighbors, sir."

"Well, I don't know about that." Wilson frowned into his glass. The prospect of meeting a crowd of new faces when he was not yet accustomed to his own was none too attractive. "I think it's a bit early to think about a party, John. I'd better get myself used to things first, don't you think? Later on, maybe."

"As you wish, Mr. Wilson. In any case," John went on, deferentially, "I thought you might want a little diversion after your trip, sir, and with that thought in mind I arranged for a model to call this afternoon for you to sketch. I hope this meets with your approval."

"Oh. Well, yes—I suppose so." Wilson yawned and set down his glass. "Will I have time for a nap?"

"You will, sir. I will awaken you at four o'clock with a tray. The model will be here at four-thirty. Her name is Sara Jane, sir."

"Good enough, John."

Wilson was in fact quite tired, but his nap was a fitful one. Several times he rose and stood smoking cigarettes by the window, staring out toward the ocean. It looked terribly empty. So did the clumps of trees and brush and the wind-swept knolls of the intervening landscape. He saw not a single bird or rabbit anywhere, nor any other living thing, and he imagined that the ocean likewise was devoid of life. Even the few residences within view, perched on the knolls, had a vacant appearance. He took some comfort in this, for it helped allay his fears that his neighbors would come to call unbidden, before he was ready to face them, but at the same time he was uneasily impressed by the emptiness of the entire scene from his window. It seemed to have no more validity than the fanciful canvases in the living room that were initialed "A.W."

When he returned to his bed to doze, his apprehensions were further heightened, for he was plagued by fantasies of a nightmarish character. Once he imagined himself in the process of demonstrating his artistic skills in public before a group of skeptical critics wearing tan cloth jackets like those of the clerks in the company's office; they jeered at his ineptitude, which was indeed appalling, for he could not manage to put his brush on the canvas, even when he began lunging desperately at it, but missed every time, greatly to his humiliation.

Thus, when John knocked and entered carrying a tray of food, Wilson awoke in a glum mood, disagreeably impressed by his situation. The company had given him a guarantee of personal freedom, it was true, but he was feeling very far removed from the exercise of his new liberty; moreover, he suspected that he would probably find it necessary to go through a further adjustment that might be fully as disturbing as the one he had recently concluded.

The arrival of Sara Jane, who seemed to be hardly more than a high school girl, did not ease his mind, either, for she began immediately to remove her clothing. He was horrified. Of course, that's what models did, but a man of his position and reputation could hardly stand idly by under such circumstances.

"Here now," he called out, dodging behind his easel. "Don't, um—"

"What's that?"

"Won't you be too—too chilly like that?"

"Heck, no. I'm used to it." She had already hung her jacket on a wire hanger in the closet and had zipped down her skirt. "Anyhow, you need a life model, don't you?"

"Well, I suppose . . ." Nervously he tested a stick of charcoal against a fresh sheet of paper tacked on the easel. He peered around the edge of the frame, feeling as though he must stop this indecent performance at once, yet not having the slightest idea of how to do so.

"I—I want to ask you something," he stammered, feeling as though he were on the verge of committing some unforgivable trespass against the modesty of this young creature, now clad only in her brassiere and pants. "What I mean," he went on, hastily, attempting to compose his features into a judicious frown, "is, um, don't you think it's a little late in the day? I mean, the light isn't too good now."

Sara Jane cocked her head inquiringly at him, meanwhile reaching around beneath one arm to find her brassiere hook. Wilson could not help noticing that despite her youth she was undeniably voluptuous, but in an awkward way, as if she had acquired the fleshly trappings of womanhood all at once, and on the previous day, so that she had not yet been able to adjust her habits of movement to the altered circumstances of her body. Still, there was nothing of discomposure in her manner. She seemed fully at her ease, with that special innocence of youth which is alarming because it implies a basis not of morality but merely of ignorance.

"You made the appointment, not me," she said, answering his question and simultaneously shrugging herself out of her brassiere.

"Yes, well. Of course, that's right."

"Want to give it a whirl, then?"

"Ah, well, I suppose I might as well."

"Okay. How's this?"

She went to a stool directly in front of the easel and perched on it with her legs crossed, her torso arched, and her head flung back dreamily.

"That's—fine."

Wilson made a few desperate strokes with his charcoal, trying to summon up memories of his art class at prep school where the pupils had sketched each other, taking turns on the stool, attired in track uniforms. But it was no good. He drew an arm which resembled a pump handle, and his memories, too, failed him, for his consciousness was wholly dominated by the prospect of young flesh before him.

He wiped his forehead. It was shameful; a man of his background ogling this girl on the pretense of being an artist. He was old enough to be her father, besides. His stick of charcoal snapped in his fingers. Hastily, as though that mishap had revealed his imposture, he picked up a fresh one and scratched away at the paper. Once more he sought to recall some of the sketching principles enunciated by the art master, but now he could not remember anything about the classroom, the students, or the master himself. It had all been long ago, and it was faded; and indeed, he thought ironically, such memories did not even belong to him now. Antiochus Wilson had no memories.

"You must be getting tired," he said at length, when he had completed his hopeless sketch.

"A little, yeah." Sara Jane stretched her arms and began to rub the back of her neck. "I'm stiff back here, mostly."

"Well, maybe that's enough for today," Wilson said cautiously. "I'm afraid I'm a bit out of practice, myself."

She eased herself off the stool. "Whatever you want. Say," she added, still kneading her neck, "this is kind of giving me a little trouble. How about your rubbing it for me some, huh?"

"Well—"

"Just loosen it up for me. Look, it'll be easier in here where I can sort of relax the other muscles." She strolled into Wilson's bedroom where she stretched herself out comfortably on the bed. "Okay?"

Wilson followed, assailed by doubts. Surely the girl must realize the implication of her action, and yet even in California there must be a law defining statutory rape. He had a vision of entrapment, accusation, prosecution and scandal . . . but against whom? Antiochus Wilson, who had practically nothing to lose.

"Um, like this?" He sat warily on the edge of the bed, his fingers gently massaging the back of her neck as she gazed up at him with her nonchalant, impersonal expression.

"Yeah, that's good." She closed her eyes contentedly, but as he simply continued to rub her neck, she reopened them and studied him for a moment. "Say, don't you want to do anything else? I mean, you're a pretty good-looking guy, you know. Like this." She sat up, embraced him firmly, and gave him a healthy kiss. "See? Don't worry about that other guy, John, I mean. He went into town when I came and he won't be back for a couple hours, so we can do whatever we want to. Play around, sort of, you and me." She began to unbutton his shirt. "It's a free country, isn't it?" She snickered, and he had the impression that she was chewing gum. "Sure, and everybody's got the right to a little fun-fun . . ."

Wilson cleared his throat. He could think of no suitable response, and so, as she continued to work at his shirt, he kissed her in return, tasting a peppermint flavor. He waited for the onset of sexual desire, but its promptings were impeded by considerations which, he tried to remind himself, were appropriate not for Antiochus Wilson, but for his obsolete predecessor. He could not banish the notion that he was engaging in some criminal molestation of an innocent minor, despite the fact that Sara Jane was obviously the aggressor in this case.

She tugged at his belt. "Come on, you help. Let's live a little," she said. He obediently removed the rest of his clothing and almost desperately plunged at her, athletically rolling about with her on the bed in a prolonged series of nuzzlings and clutchings which, however, did not quite result in a certain necessary effect.

"I'm sorry. Wait a minute." He stopped trying and

sat up nervously, reaching for his cigarettes. The room was brilliant with late afternoon light; he felt that their tumblings had been exposed to public view through the great windows, and yet there was nothing outside. He could see the blank sky, the vacant ocean, the naked roll of land that was spotted with brush and houses which appeared empty of life. He was exposed—to nothingness. What was wrong?

She was talking to him and tickling him suggestively. He stared down at her. " . . . Never say die, that's my motto." Her voice was matter-of-fact. "I mean, nobody's perfect. Rome wasn't built in a day. How about my getting some clothes on, and then you can sort of take them off me again. Maybe—"

"No, please. Just let me—smoke for a minute." He looked away once more. She popped her gum.

"You've got to understand," he said finally, "that I'm in an unusual state of mind. Everything's strange to me. I've been thrown suddenly from one kind of world into another, quite different, and I'm having to discover myself as a person, as a man, all over again, do you see?"

"No kidding."

"It's hard to explain," he began, but he went no further. The faint movement of her jaws as she secretly manipulated her gum seemed somehow to constitute an insuperable obstacle to communication, even if he had clearly in mind what he wished to express. "Nothing," he said.

"Well, look. I'll come back tomorrow."

"I'm not sure about tomorrow. Why don't you wait for John to get in touch with you."

"Okay." She shrugged her shoulders and lazily climbed off the bed. "You sure you wouldn't like to play around some more for fun-fun?"

"Not today, but thank you anyway. It's not your fault."

"Okay."

He felt ridiculous sitting there uttering conventional remarks, as if Sara Jane were someone who had come to his office to inquire about an account. She left him; he saw in the mirror on the closet door opposite a lean, almost satyrlike man sitting cross-legged on a bed, nude, and smoking a cigarette. He waved to the stranger, who simultaneously waved back and grinned at him sarcastically. From the studio, he could hear Sara Jane whistling as she got dressed.

That would be the end of life sketches, he decided, until . . . well, until he managed to turn himself into the bona fide Antiochus Wilson, whom he imagined as a fairly rakish and casual man of the world, capable of ravishing a dozen young models without the slightest qualm. In the meantime, he knew he must make certain temporary concessions to his bankerish soul. After all, it stood to reason that the habits of nearly five decades could not be rooted out overnight.

"No more Sara Jane, John."

"Very good, sir."

"Actually, you see, I'm in the process of redefining my approach, um, to my painting, and I won't be needing live models at present. She's a good model, though. I trust she won't suffer from the loss of my business."

"I doubt that she will, sir."

"No, I suppose she won't."

"Perhaps you'd be interested later on in some more mature models, Mr. Wilson?"

"N-no, I don't think so, John."

"Are you sure you wouldn't like me to arrange that little cocktail party for the neighborhood people—?"

"Not yet, John. Not yet . . ."

For several days he lounged around the house, conscientiously spending hours in his studio practicing at the easel. He tried puttering in the garden, too, but the plants there were unfamiliar to him, spiny and sparse-leaved growths with little beauty. They did not seem to welcome care. Sometimes he lay on a lounge chair on the rear terrace, an unopened book in his lap, feeling the sun flow down on him.

Vastness enveloped him: the unrelieved blue of the sky, the great stare of the sun, the open and endless stretch of ocean far away, and the mindless horizons of his own slow thoughts. He longed, suddenly, for the confinement of his commuter train, for the jostling of crowded streets, for the close desk-clutter of a busy day; but once in the midst of these yearnings when he heard a car pull into the driveway in front, he leaped up in fright from his chair and fled inside to his room, emerging only when it became clear that the visitor was merely a deliveryman from the grocery.

He paced up and down before a mirror, glancing severely at his image from time to time. It was shameful to slink around in such a cowardly fashion, he told himself. He couldn't avoid meeting people forever by hiding in his house. He owed it to himself to act like a man—that was the crux of the matter. Besides, the monetary investment he had made in his rebirth demanded that he obtain a fair return.

He stopped in front of the mirror and shook his finger sternly at the image. Yet it was no craven creature that confronted him there, but instead a handsome and self-possessed man of the world, ironic and knowing, with a slightly lecherous twist to one corner of the mouth. Wilson gaped at the reflection—and the gape became, almost magically, a satanic leer. My God, he thought, that's me. He strode nervously about again and paused once more at the glass. Again, he was filled with wonder at the renewed consciousness of what the company had wrought. He swelled his chest and flexed his muscles, watching in fascination the subtle play of expression on the face of Antiochus Wilson. There seemed to be a remarkable disparity between his own emotions and what was reflected in the features of the image. The timidity he felt was nowhere evident in the attitude of the man in the mirror, and in fact it—that is to say, *he*—appeared as bold as a lion; indeed, the longer he examined himself, the less timid he felt, and the more confident the figure looked to him, until finally he had the impression that if he remained transfixed much longer, he would rush out of the house and commit the Lord knew what acts of libertinism.

He turned from the mirror, still tingling with self-approbation. No more creeping and cringing, that was clear. No more hiding, either. He swaggered from the room—"I'm off to the beach, John!"—and headed out toward the car.

He drove recklessly along the route John had previously indicated to him, wishing that he were behind the wheel of one of those little European sports cars instead of a mere sedan. When he arrived at the beach, he changed into his trunks outside the car, despite the fact that the beach was not completely deserted, and that at least one of the bathers within view was a woman. But at that moment, still in the thrall of his vision of himself, Wilson cared not a bit for conventional morality. He laughed aloud, and before leaving the car he took one last look in the rear-vision mirror on the side. "You devil," he muttered, cheerfully.

He flung down his towel and sprinted into the water, plunging and snorting as he fought the waves. He was irked, however, to discover that he had neglected to remove his wristwatch. Moreover, the coldness of the water quickly took the edge off his high spirits, and in addition to that, he experienced a painful twinge in his lower back; it reminded him that he was not, after all, a youngster of twenty, and so, somewhat chastened, he emerged and plodded across the sand to his towel.

There were only six figures visible along the great curve of beach. The nearest was a woman who was sketching with a pencil on a large pad. She was not at all bad-looking, Wilson thought; her figure was good, too, and it seemed to him besides that she had cast a couple of glances in his direction. He wondered whether he should saunter over. The banker within him counseled caution, but the memories of the man in the mirror were still fresh in his mind, and so he rose to his feet, lighted a cigarette, and obeyed the predominant impulse.

"You're sketching, I see," he declared—and was shaken by the realization that although his appearance was that of a rakehell, the words would necessarily be those of the banker.

But the woman was not repelled by the inanity of his remark. She smiled up at him invitingly. "Oh, yes," she said. "I sometimes do a little drawing just to pass the time." She put the pad aside.

"Oh, please go on," he said. "I don't want to interrupt you." He craned his neck, pretending to admire the latticework of lines that represented a meeting of sea and sky, wondering how a man of the world would proceed to develop the situation. Perhaps he ought to sit beside her; but he reflected that she might consider this too forward, and so he stood uncomfortably pondering the problem, until she asked him if he wouldn't like to sit down.

"Thank you very much," he said. As he sat, however, the twinge in his back reasserted itself, and he became increasingly aware of the divergence between his exterior and interior selves. He wished he had brought along a pocket mirror to peek at once in a while, to renew his confidence, but he supposed that even if he had, the woman would think it odd of him.

"I sketch a little myself," he remarked, for the sake of conversation.

"Oh—then I shouldn't even let you look at what I've done," the woman exclaimed, and coquettishly moved as if to turn her drawing pad over.

"No, really," said Wilson, "you're very good." He politely motioned to forestall her. Their hands touched. She glanced at him, not with hauteur but with a bold calculation, letting her fingers slide slowly, as if by accident, across his wrist.

Wilson was alarmed. He had no idea of what to do. He longed to leave. And yet at the same time he strongly suspected that his features were communicating a formidable impression of lustful intentions. He was trapped, a sheep in wolf's clothing.

"Wouldn't you like to take a dip?" he inquired.

"Oh, but the water's so cold." She sighed deeply, not so much to indicate her disinclination to swim, Wilson feared, as to demonstrate the fullness of her bosom. "Anyway," she added, "I have to go back to my cottage and fix my lunch."

The feeling of relief that swept over him at this announcement was short-lived, however, for the woman made no move to pick up her things, but remained curled languorously at his side, gazing at him.

"Is it, um, far?" he asked, politely.

"A few miles." She sighed again, more deeply this time; Wilson turned his head.

"Look at those gulls!" he exclaimed enthusiastically, pointing to a pair of specks a mile away.

She paid no attention to the gulls. "The place belongs to a friend of mine, actually," she continued, letting a handful of sand trickle teasingly across his forearm. "I borrow it once in a while for a few days. It's nice to get off sometimes all by yourself, don't you think?"

"Absolutely," Wilson responded, with caution.

"No one around to bother you," she went on. "Just complete quiet and peace. Not even a telephone, and no neighbors or anything."

"That sounds fine."

"And it's such a clean, simple little place. Just a stove and an icebox, that's all. And a bed."

Wilson's spirits sank further still. There could be no mistaking her intentions now. He tried to gather his courage by examining all that he could see of himself—his sinewy arms and legs—and turned his head bravely to face her again.

She was smiling with an air of sensual complicity, her eyebrows suggestively arched, waiting for the Lothario at her side to make the obvious suggestion—a little lunch together.

But he only mumbled: "It all sounds—cosy."

"Yes, it is." She fluttered her eyelids at him.

He felt suddenly betrayed. What right did the company have to manufacture a façade for him that was so completely at odds with his inner nature? He should have been given the opportunity to choose a more moderate version.

"Well," she said, "I guess I'd better be on my way." For the first time, she seemed a little vexed. She gathered up her pad and pencils slowly, occasionally glancing at him.

He did not dare even to smile politely, for fear his alien face would transform the smile into a wolfish leer and again inspire her advances.

She stood up finally, brushing off the sand. He stood, too, and to avoid her gaze pretended to take great interest in his sodden wristwatch.

"I'm afraid it's stopped," he said.

"Maybe it never got started," she snapped; without another word she marched off, a woman scorned.

Wilson sat down again, humbly staring out at the ocean. He took the back off the watch, to inspect its works, but it slipped from his fingers into the sand. In despair, he let it remain where it had fallen, thinking that it was probably now beyond repair.

In a little while, he walked over to pick up his towel and plodded back toward his car, peering around for signs of his frustrated companion. She was nowhere in sight, but just as he was about to climb into the car, he heard his name called out by someone behind him.

Wilson turned, in surprise. A little man wearing a loud Hawaiian shirt above his trunks was standing some twenty paces away, his hand upraised in greeting.

"Good to see you back with us, Tony," the man cried. He started to walk toward the car, but Wilson leaped inside, started the engine with feverish haste, backed away, turned, and drove off at top speed. His earlier doubts and fancies were most powerfully revived. The salutation of the beefy man at the airport, which he had dismissed as coincidence, now assumed a more sinister aspect, as did even the airline stewardess's inquiry as to whether he had been her passenger before.

He went at once to his room, where he changed out of his trunks and lay down. He thought of summoning John, but he was quivering from head to toe, and he decided it would be unwise to confront his servant until his agitation had abated. Sitting up, he sought the reassurance of the mirror on the closet door, but the sight did not allay his anxiety, for he seemed to be looking not at the image of himself, but into an adjoining room, where a stranger sat on another bed, eyeing him sardonically.

He thought of taking a drink, a trip, of growing a beard and hiding away somewhere in the mountains. The woman had been bad enough, in emphasizing the difference between what he seemed and what he was, but if the implication of the little man's familiarity proved correct, then what?

That evening he was still upset, but nonetheless he was determined to have matters out with John once and for all.

"Look here, John," he began. "Things can't go on

like this." He described his disturbing encounter with the man at the beach, and reminded John of the similar episode at the airport. "It's a damned outrage," he declared. "There seem to be people who know *me*, but at the same time I don't know *them*."

"I see, sir."

"No, you don't see. How can you see? You've never been in this position," Wilson complained, pacing to and fro in the living room. "Do you understand what this kind of thing suggests, John? By God, I have this peculiar feeling, wondering if some day I won't turn a corner and come face to face with myself. Now, seriously," Wilson declared, shaking a finger in John's face, "we've got to find some way out of this mess. Tell me frankly, John—is there or isn't there another Antiochus Wilson? I think I have a right to know."

"You need reassurance, sir."

"You're damned right I do."

"But unfortunately, Mr. Wilson, I'm in no position personally to satisfy you," John added. "If you will be willing to wait for a while, though, perhaps I can arrange something."

"Like what?"

"I'm sorry, sir, but if you will be patient—"

"All right, John," Wilson grumbled. "Do it your way. I don't want to pry into your affairs, but it seems to me that they're my affairs, too. After all, I've spent a good deal of money and gone to a lot of trouble to get to my present position, and it's no bed of roses, either," he added, thinking of his perplexity at the problem of dealing with the all-too-willing woman at the beach, "and to have this anxiety on top of it all, is just too damned much. Do you see what I mean?"

"Completely, sir."

"I hope so, John."

"Very good, sir," muttered John, who then left with a troubled expression.

Wilson went outside to the terrace. The night was bland and moist, for a fog was moving in from the ocean. There was no odor in the air; no fragrance of flowers, no resinous aroma of trees, not even the freshness of sea salt. All was temperate and damp, and as the fog became more dense, it obscured the random lights that marked the neighboring houses until they were no more than greyish patches in a wet black cavern that seemed to be slowly circling. A new world, Wilson thought. A new life. Of course it was bound to be alarming, he told himself. What else could be expected, when he had so suddenly cast off all of the old associations and memories on which he had become accustomed to depend? Any man would find such an experience quite difficult. But of course that did not exactly cover the particular problem that was uppermost in his mind. If there were another Antiochus Wilson, then the company would stand convicted either of gross carelessness or downright fraud. He was in the process of wondering whether he should not take the precaution in any case of consulting a lawyer when his meditations were interrupted by John's voice, summoning him inside.

"A long-distance call for you, sir."

"Eh? Oh, yes."

But who would be calling him? Nervously, he approached the telephone. He knew no one. Almost literally, he knew no one.

"Um, hello?"

It was Charley. Wilson sighed in relief.

"My God, Charley, if you knew how good it is to hear a familiar voice!"

"Look here, old boy. I understand you've got a case of nerves. That's why I'm calling. And by the way," Charley went on, "I guess I'd better call you Wilson. All right?"

"Of course; but listen, Charley—"

"You don't have to tell me your situation. I know all about it. I mean, I know what's troubling you. Well, I can tell you, old boy, your fears are quite groundless. Believe me, this comes from the highest authority. I can guarantee that you are the absolute and only Antiochus Wilson in existence."

"Thank God for that."

"Feel better now?"

"Of course I do, Charley. But that still doesn't explain why some people around here seem to know me."

"Well, that's a bit more complicated. There's an explanation, all right, and actually the company made a little miscalculation in your case, and I'll explain that, too. But tell me, apart from this one worry you've had, how've things been going?"

"Frankly," said Wilson, "they haven't gone too well.

I'm completely at sea on this thing, Charley. I haven't got my bearings yet. Believe me, it would help me tremendously to see you again. Can't we arrange to get together? Where are you now, for example?"

"I'm afraid that'll be impossible at present," said Charley. "I couldn't get away." He hesitated. "Anyway, we wouldn't exactly recognize each other now, you understand," he added, more slowly, "and that might not be what the doctor ordered, in your present mental attitude. You need friends, naturally. But you'll find them, old boy. You'll find them."

Wilson remained silent.

"You're just a little jumpy right now," Charley continued. "But let me try to give you a little perspective. That's one thing you need—perspective. Are you with me?"

"Yes."

"Look at it this way. You're living a dream. All those longings you had back in the old days—well, they've come true now. You've got what almost every middle-aged man in America would like to have. Freedom. Real freedom. You can do any damned thing you want to. You've got financial security, you've got no responsibilities, and you've got no reason at all to feel guilty about what you've done. The company's taken care of everything. Right?"

"I suppose so."

"Of course you're anxious. But that'll pass. You're a pioneer, old boy. That's literally true. The old frontier, you know what that was? That was a dream, too. A new life, a new chance. Out on the prairies, in the mountains, wherever there were empty spaces for men to start over again. Well, that's finished. We'll never have that again. But there's a different frontier now—the frontier of personal freedom, and I mean *real* freedom—and there are different pioneers, too. You're one of 'em, Wilson, and all I can say is that pioneering is no easy trick in any man's language, but the rewards are tremendous. Tremendous."

"I sincerely hope so."

"It's the wave of the future," Charley went on, expansively. "I'm no damned sociologist, but you know as well as I do that we've got what the professors call an 'open society.' Well, to me, that means mobility. A man can move toward what he wants, regardless of class or creed. It doesn't matter who his parents were or how he votes or what church he goes to. You know what I mean? What I'm trying to say is that the company has broken through the last important barrier to true mobility, and I suppose if you had to give that barrier a name, you'd call it identity. Most people can change a lot of things—their church, their political party, their place of residence—but they can't change their identity. Well, *we* did. That's the difference. That's the big difference. By God, Wilson, I don't want to preach at you, but I think you can make a darned good case for the idea that we represent a future America. Naturally," Charley added, clearing his throat, "it took a lot of money in our cases, but I wouldn't be at all surprised if in a few years this process became available to everyone, including those of moderate means."

"Have they thought of the installment plan?"

Charley chuckled. "By God, it's good to know you've still got your sense of humor. I guess your spirits aren't as droopy as you thought, eh? But actually, you may have a point there. Once the company gets all the wrinkles out of its techniques, then maybe they'll want to reach a bigger market and reduce unit costs. But I guess they aren't ready for that yet."

"Speaking of wrinkles, you said the company made a miscalculation in my case."

"Oh. Well, in most instances, the company is anxious to have its clients completely absorbed in their new identities. Forget the old life, accept the new—do you follow me? Well, this isn't too simple sometimes, because although the exterior is different, the client's mind is the same, and maybe he hangs on to his past a little too strongly. If this was Russia, old boy, there'd be some brainwashing to take care of that problem, but thank God, this is a free country and we don't indulge in that sort of thing. But as I was saying, the company's whole position is that psychologically the client must be encouraged to believe that he has never been anybody but the person he has suddenly become. Is that clear? It's supposed to speed up the process of getting used to the new identity, you see. So one of the tactics is to imply the existence of a past that doesn't really exist, but logically ought to—is this confusing, old boy?"

"No. But if this means having total strangers come up and clap you on the back like an old friend, Charley, all that does is scare the life out of you. It did me, anyhow."

"Well, as I said, the company miscalculated with you. You're too sensitive for that kind of conditioning, evidently."

"Who are these men, then? Did the company hire a bunch of actors or what?"

"They're not actors, Wilson. Not exactly, no. They're more or less like you are."

"What do you mean?"

Charley sighed, as if he feared making any disclosures over the long-distance telephone system.

"Like you, Wilson. Um, pioneers."

"You mean they're reborns, too?"

"That's it. In a word, they were briefed on your arrival and instructed to greet you as an old friend. Obviously, this was an error."

"So they don't really know me."

"Of course not."

"Well, that takes a load off my mind. But I wonder why the hell my servant didn't tell me about this."

"Not authorized, old boy."

Wilson hesitated. "But listen, Charley," he said, "how many of these people are there around here? I've hardly had my nose outside since I've been out here, and I've already run into two of them."

"Actually, there are quite a few. You're living in a kind of colony of them, old man. You get your servant to have a party. Get acquainted. You'll find them a likable crowd. You've got plenty in common."

"But the women, are they—?"

"Oh, no. Just the men. The women aren't involved, and naturally this is the kind of thing you don't tell anybody about, even your wife, not that anyone would believe it. Well, the women are wives or the equivalent and a nice lively bunch of girls, too, as I understand it, and I'm sure you can get yourself acclimated in that department, too."

"But wait a minute. You mean *all* the men around here are like me?"

"Probably. Most, anyway."

"But some aren't? How'm I supposed to know?"

"Old boy," said Charley, firmly. "It isn't supposed to make any difference. You ignore it, understand?"

"That's all very well to say, Charley, but look here. Suppose I meet some fellow who's got a Harvard degree. Maybe he was in my class, even. Well, dammit, how am I supposed to know whether he really was or not? It can't be proved either way, if you see what I mean."

"Old boy," said Charley again, more firmly. "You didn't go to Harvard."

"The hell I didn't."

"You better refresh your memory, my friend. There was a fellow I once knew who went to Harvard, but he died of a stroke several months ago. Do you get me?"

Wilson winced. "All right. Yes. But you've got to admit it's confusing, all this."

"Sure it is," said Charley, in a more soothing tone. "Now listen. I've been on this call too long. I think

I've explained the basic situation to you and I hope I've cleared away your worries. You just keep paddling away, old boy, and sooner than you think you'll really begin to enjoy life—every single minute, every single day. That's what you paid for, that's what the company contracted to deliver, and that's what you're going to get. Now you get your servant to throw a little party and you start making friends. A man needs friends, and believe me, the fellows out around you are totally sympathetic to your position, and they'll do everything they can to make you feel at ease. The company's passed the word about their little mistake, and this 'old friend' stuff will definitely be soft-pedaled from now on. Okay?"

"Sure, Charley."

"And you feel better now, don't you?"

"I can't thank you enough. I really can't. But look, Charley, let me have your phone number, in case—"

"So long, old boy," said Charley, in a cheerful voice, and there was a definitive click at the end of the line.

The cocktail party was held five days later. John handled all of the arrangements, sending out invitations, hiring additional servants for the occasion, and leaving nothing for Wilson to do but study the guest list, where beside each name John had helpfully noted the person's physical characteristics and occupation.

Dutifully, Wilson studied the list, virtually committing it to memory. All of the men, he saw, were "about

40," and all of them, too, were engaged in rather vague occupations. There were several investment analysts, which could mean almost anything; a few were writers, and some were listed as "commercial representatives," or "industrial consultants," while one was frankly identified as "retired." Wilson supposed that this last man represented a failure on the part of the company's guidance adviser, Mr. Davalo. Yet wouldn't it be simpler, he thought, for all the clients to be considered as retired? That's what they were, surely. And then, too, why was he so compulsively studying the list of guests, when every item of information on it was meaningless, in the sense that all had been artifically created by the physicians and technicians of the company back East? John had written "bald spot" beside the name of a Mr. Filter, but that attribute was undoubtedly a subtle refinement sketched on Filter's scalp in the Delivery Room some few short months ago; and what if that gentleman were questioned rather closely on his supposed specialty of investment analysis . . . would he fumble for answers and grow embarrassed and seek to find some other topic of conversation?

However, Wilson firmly dismissed from his mind such impertinent speculations—after all, he himself would be equally vulnerable in matters of art—and determined to carry out his responsibilities as host in good faith. At least the women were bona fide, he reflected. Some were wives, according to John's list, while others were merely noted delicately as "friend" of the gentlemen they were to accompany. There were, all together, twenty-four men and women. Quite a crowd for him to manage by himself, Wilson thought, and he suddenly wished that Emily were with him for the occasion. Despite her failings, she was a skillful hostess and invariably had undertaken the management of all the bores and drunks and lechers who had attended their parties in Connecticut. John, of course, would take care of the canapés and the drinks, but for the rest of it—the small talk, the maneuvering of groups, the instinct for anticipating trouble spots—a woman was absolutely necessary. Wilson wondered: should he ask John to engage some mature lady for the evening? Surely there were women who did this sort of thing. Then he recalled that John's previous choice of female companionship for him had not been too successful, and so he decided not to risk making matters worse. He would face his guests alone.

On the afternoon of the party, Wilson's resolution weakened. He realized that for months he had been virtually a recluse. How well would he stand up to the inspection of all these people? To ease his anxiety, he took a quick drink, and when that did not seem to have much effect, he poured himself a second one which he sipped in his bathroom as he shaved. While he dressed, he conscientiously renewed his study of the guest list, feeling somewhat heartened by the warmth of the whiskey.

"Filter, short with bald spot," he chanted to the mirror as he tied his tie. "Mayberry, tall and thin. Call him Bill." He winked at his image. "R. L. Hamrick, ruddy with horn-rims," he continued. "Phil Jolson and wife Sandra, stout and purple." No, not purple—purposeful. He snickered at his error. But what right did John have to call anyone purposeful? What purpose could this Mr. Jolson have, anyway, except to remain at "about age 40"?

Wilson took one more drink just before the guests were to arrive, and managed to receive them in a condition of perfect cordiality, for although he was a triffle lightheaded, his speech was not blurred and he was in control of his gestures. The men and women came in a rush, as if they all had alighted from some enormous car, and Wilson found himself besieged by hands and furs and perfumes. He forgot the guest list, but he felt it did not matter. The gaiety of the voices surrounding him encouraged him to believe that at last he was among decent and happy people who would in time become his good friends. He had seen two of them before—the Texan who had so alarmed him at the airport, and the man who had been at the beach—but now they did not represent threats, of course, and as if to show there were no hard feelings, he personally conducted them to the portable bar John had set up near the hearth.

He returned to the door to greet the stragglers, and saw among them a woman he knew—knew from a past that had been all but surgically removed from him in the creation of his new identity. In that instant of recognition, his pose as Wilson seemed exploded by this one quick pinprick of familiarity. He was exposed.

His ears roared with the buzzing of some interior derision as he advanced, trembling, to greet her. It was, by some impudent turn of irony, his good friend Charley's wife, Sue, and his astonishment was too great to be repressed.

"My God—Sue!"

Sue was not at all disconcerted, but came toward him coquettishly, with a gay appraising look in her eye. "Well!" she exclaimed, taking his hand, "and so you're mine host!"

"What are you doing here?"

"You invited me. I think. Anyway, I'm here," she declared brightly. Then she hesitated. "Am I supposed to know you from somewhere?" she asked dubiously, taking a swift inventory of her recollections, for Sue was a woman with a voluminous past and a short memory. "I swear I can't place you, Mr. Wilson," she added, "and now that I've had a chance to look you over, I'm honestly sorry about it." She giggled and grasped his arm firmly. "But you come on and meet my husband now," she continued, nodding her head toward a lanky gentleman who was handing his hat to John. "He plays golf every Tuesday and Thursday afternoons, Tony—it is Tony, isn't it?—and he'd love to have you join his foursome, or whatever he calls it. And if you don't play golf, why then maybe there's something else you'd like to do on Tuesday and Thursday afternoons," she declared, massaging his arm, "like maybe make a twosome somewhere. Oh, Henry," she called to her husband, "look what I found in the foyer!

Our host, Mr. Wilson. Tony, meet Henry. Henry Bushbane. My husband," Sue confided to Wilson as the two men shook hands, "is supposed to be a writer, but he doesn't write and he sure can't spell." She giggled, still clutching Wilson's arm. "He can't spell his own name half the time!"

"Darling," protested Mr. Bushbane, with the same look of gloomy foreboding Wilson had seen so often on Charley's face.

"Let me show you to the bar," said Wilson. He had by this time recovered his composure. Good Lord, he thought, he had almost been betrayed by the sight of Sue into making a terrible gaffe. It was pure coincidence, her being married to one of the reborns. But it was bigamy, too, wasn't it, since Charley hadn't killed himself after all? No matter. Poor Bushbane.

"Here we are," said Wilson cheerily. "Name it, Bushbane. We've got it. I think," he added, as he got a further glimpse of Sue wriggling up to someone else's husband, like some disreputable evidence of the past which had escaped the company's notice, "I'll have one, too."

He had two, and then a third . . . or was it a fourth? Anyway, it seemed to help. He chattered small talk effortlessly, and moved from group to group, smiling, laughing, getting names mixed up but not caring—being, in short, an almost perfect host, and even receiving occasional glances of grave approval from John.

An hour passed. The room seemed terribly crowded, full of smoke and laughter. Someone sat down unexpectedly in the tiny fountain in the center of the conversation pit. It was Sue Bushbane.

A plump blonde wearing thick glasses was mooing softly at Wilson's shoulder for attention. "Don't you just love it out here?" she was saying.

"Oh, California. Absolutely." Wilson cast a host's eye toward the conversation pit. Sue sat squealing merrily atop the fountain, her skirt darkening; but no one seemed to mind. He shrugged and gave the blonde a complacent smile. "Delightful climate," he added.

"There's something religious about it, don't you agree?"

"In a sense—"

"I mean all these religious groups out here, the kinds you just don't find back East," the blonde explained.

"You certainly don't."

"I belong to a special kind of group," she went on, pressing his arm earnestly. "We change sects."

"I beg your pardon."

"Each month, we change sects. The one we're in now, the basic belief is reincarnation." She simpered, then frowned at her glass, as if the liquor had betrayed her into worldliness. "You know, spirits investing one body after the other, as part of the great Unknowable. Mr. Wilson, do you think there's anything to that?"

"I'm afraid I couldn't say," said Wilson. He laughed. "I'm sorry," he said, but laughed again. She blinked at him doubtfully, and to avoid the threat of more laughter, he reached out and tapped the shoulder of the nearest man. "Um, Mr. Jolson here," he told her, "I understand he's well informed on things like that—aren't you, Jolson?"

"Mayberry," muttered the man.

Wilson freed his arm from the blonde, at the same time maneuvering her to face Mayberry. "The Reverend Mayberry," he whispered puckishly in her ear. "Mayberry," he declared, "this young woman has a theory about reincarnation that ought to be of interest to every man in the room." He chuckled and winked broadly at Mayberry, but instead of winking back in acknowledgment of the irony, Mayberry stiffened, pursed his lips, and looked decidedly ill at ease. Old sourpuss, thought Wilson. What harm could there be in a little joke?

"Reincarnation," he repeated, mischievously. He pressed the blonde forward. "New bodies for old souls, isn't that right, my dear?"

But without waiting for her reply, he edged away, leaving Mayberry to deal with her. "Reincarnation," he said again, to no one, but from across the room he caught a calculating glance from one of the men, as if his exchange with Mayberry had violated some secret code of behavior which had been immediately sensed by the brotherhood. It did not bother him; rather, he was suddenly struck by the amusing notion that he was present at a masquerade whose social façade, ostensibly so proper and ordinary, would at any moment be thrown into confusion with the ripping off of masks and the beginning of wild dancing. The thought made him feel reckless and gay. He snapped his fingers in the air and snatched up another drink. Masks off! Why not?

"I'm crazy about your painting, you know that?" remarked Mrs. Filter, a dark little woman he found himself wedged close to in a corner. "How do you ever do it, anyway?"

"I paint stark naked. That's the only way to get at the truth."

"My God, of course."

"You ought to try it."

"I'll try anything once," she said, significantly. A heavy-set man backed into her. "Hey—oh, it's my husband. Joe," she said to him, "we've got to have Mr. Wilson over for dinner sometime soon, you know that?"

"Of course." Mr. Filter, however, seemed slightly annoyed at the sight of his wife on such familiar terms with Wilson, for she in fact had one arm around Wilson's waist. "Next week, maybe? Not that we want to interfere with your artistic labors, Wilson," he added, with a touch of sarcasm that irked Wilson.

"I'll make time," Wilson responded coldly. "What about your own crowded work schedule?"

"Joe's an investment analyst," Mrs. Filter explained.

"Oh? But what do you really do?" Wilson asked the man. "Or should I say what *did* you do?"

"I'm afraid I don't understand," said Filter, giving him a sharp glance of warning, but at this point Wilson noticed that Sue Bushbane was playfully splashing water on the other guests in the conversation pit, and he disengaged himself from Mrs. Filter to attend to her.

"You'll weaken their drinks," he told Sue, and then, to command her attention, launched a dubious subject. "I knew your first husband, Charley. Um, whatever became of him?"

She stood up, dripping, and gaped at him. "Oh— him. It was terrible." She giggled. "I'm sorry, it really was awful. We went to this island for a vacation. I forget the name, but it had this crater on it. You know, a kind of volcano. Right in the middle, smoking away, and all the tourists were supposed to go see it, but it gave me a headache so I didn't go up, but Charley did, poor boy, and he went into it."

"He fell?"

"He jumped or fell or something, but you see he took his coat off before and left it on the edge, so they called it suicide and I couldn't collect double on the insurance. But I can't believe he meant to do it. Charley had everything to live for, don't you think so?" she asked archly, edging closer to him.

"But surely someone saw what happened."

"Well, yes, a lot of people did, but he went around to the smoky side, where people weren't supposed to go, so nobody could tell exactly whether he took a nose dive or just slipped, do you see? They *saw* him fall in, but it was too smoky to see just how, and so there was nothing clear-cut for the insurance people to go on, which is why I think it was really an accident, because

Charley was such a methodical man, you know. He always had a reason for everything. But it was terrible for me, you know," she added, blinking her eyes as if about to weep. "There I was on vacation all alone, with another week to go and not knowing a soul, except for a nice man named Joliffe who'd sat at our table a couple of times. He saw Charley go, too, and he was considerate enough to try to help me get over the shock. Oh, I was absolutely prostrated," she added, and then, as though her phrase had recalled an image of a different character, she giggled. "But where did you get to know Charley, anyhow?"

"Oh—at college. We were classmates at Harvard."

"Really? Say, that's something." She grabbed the sleeve of a passing gentleman and tugged him around to face Wilson. "This is Bobby Hamrick. Bobby went to Harvard, too, didn't you, Bobby?"

"Um, that's right," said Mr. Hamrick, uncertainly.

"Your house wasn't Adams, by any chance?" inquired Wilson, before it occurred to him that Mr. Hamrick's Harvard background would be of synthetic origin.

"Adams? Well, no, not exactly—"

"I'm sorry," Wilson added quickly, anxious to cover his faux pas. "I forgot. I didn't mean to pry. Actually," he went on, aware that the liquor had given him a heedless tongue, "I'm not a Harvard alumnus, either— *myself*, I mean to say. That is, I *used* to be, but I'm not any more." This explanation somehow did not seem to be satisfactory, for Mr. Hamrick was now glaring at him in a forbidding manner. Sue Bushbane, clinging to his arm, was greatly amused.

"What do you mean," she cried out, "did you resign or something? My God, that's priceless."

"No," Wilson went on, honestly determined to come up with some convincing reason to repair his mistake, "I *did* go to Harvard, you see, and I *was* an alumnus, but that was a long time ago, before I became a painter, and now—now I'm not any more." The incongruity of his situation struck him as being quite funny. He laughed, and the sight of Hamrick's face, thunderously grave and fairly rippling with unspoken admonitions, made him laugh all the harder. It was just like old Filter, the pseudo investment analyst, Wilson thought, and sure enough, there was Filter not too far away, reinforcing Hamrick's silent signals with those of his own.

"The truth is," Wilson spluttered, "that I just stopped being an alumnus. It's that simple." He gave Hamrick a playful punch on the shoulder. "Haven't you ever stopped anything, for example?"

Hamrick closed in on him. "We must play golf together sometime, Wilson," he said, meaningfully. Filter had approached from the other side, and Wilson saw several other men moving slowly his way.

"Golf," Hamrick repeated, taking his arm.

"Did you learn golf at Harvard, Hamrick?" asked Wilson gaily, but as he saw that his irreverent attitude was causing his guests real concern, he composed himself. "I'm sorry," he said. "My tongue just keeps on wagging. Look." He stuck his tongue out and wagged it. "But don't worry, gentlemen, I'll try to keep myself in check. There's just one question on my mind, and I'll be satisfied." He turned to Hamrick. "Where *did* you go to college, old boy? I mean, was it Yale or Columbia . . . ?" The group of men around him had sprouted hands, and the hands were gently edging Wilson in the direction of his bedroom. He did not resist, for he realized that his lack of control had created a certain problem in etiquette, but his voice continued anyway. "I'd really like to know, Hamrick, because if it was Columbia, I've got a cousin who went there, about your time, and you might remember the name. And come to think of it, by God, I've got a nephew who's there right now, at the law school—"

"You don't have a nephew," someone whispered angrily. Wilson was conscious of having left the living room and that John was among those who were guiding him to bed.

"You're damn' right," he conceded. "I forgot." He was seated on the bed. Someone was removing his shoes. "I don't have a nephew. You're right there. But anyway, he's at Columbia, and my daughter—I mean, I realize I don't have a daughter—but my daughter, she's married to a doctor and maybe by this time— who knows?—she's got a baby. Do you know that? By God, John," he continued, addressing the nearest face, "I might be a grandfather by now. Isn't that something? I mean, if I *had* a daughter, which I'm the first to admit that I don't, of course." He leaned dizzily backward, gazing uncertainly at the figures surrounding the bed who were examining him with what he sensed was deep reproach. "Never fear, gentlemen," he declared, attempting to reassure them. "I am perfectly aware of the facts. If I am a grandfather, believe me, they'll never drag it out of me, not even in court . . ." And with this, he clapped both hands to his throbbing head and burst into prolonged laughter.

CHAPTER 4

He did not tell John where he was going. He told no one. Indeed, he himself did not seem to have decided finally on his destination until he marched up to the airport ticket counter, his suitcase in his hand, and in response to the clerk's inquiry, mumbled: "Denver."

"One-way?"

"No, round-trip, please."

He checked his bag and went into the bar to wait for his flight to be called. In the mirror, his face appeared pale and puffy among the reflected bottles and the shuttling figure of the bartender. The mirror's image of an illuminated clock on the opposite wall showed the hands reversed, with time retreating. For reassurance, he glanced at his wristwatch. Yes, in four hours he would be in Denver, and from there it would be but an hour's drive to his daughter's house. It was not to see her again that he was going, he told himself, but simply . . . well, for one thing, he wanted to make sure that she had gotten her portion of his estate, because if a baby were on the way, there would be added expenses, and her husband was probably not making much yet, being so recently out of medical school. Of course, he couldn't just barge in and inquire bluntly about money matters; he would have to hint around a little.

"Hello, Wilson."

It was Henry Bushbane, who had climbed up on the next stool. Wilson flushed guiltily and cleared his throat. "Ah. Bushbane."

"Going somewhere, Wilson?"

"Er, yes, as a matter of fact, I am. I thought," said Wilson, craftily, "I'd take in some of the night life at Las Vegas. I've never been there, but I've heard a lot about it." He sensed that Bushbane was regarding him with a certain air of irony, as if he knew full well Wilson's real intentions. Somewhat defiantly, Wilson added: "And what about yourself?"

"Oh, I'm not going anywhere." Bushbane smiled sadly and gave his order to the bartender.

There was an uneasy pause. Bushbane turned around to study the entrance for a moment, and then, when his drink had been placed before him, he winked at Wilson and said: "Let's go back to a booth, what do you say? They can spot us too easily here."

"Who can?" Wilson asked, but he followed Bushbane to a booth anyway, where they sat in semi-darkness while soft piped music hummed at them from a hidden loudspeaker. The room was decorated in heavy shades of green, which gave Bushbane's face an even more saturnine cast.

"Look here, Wilson," Bushbane began, "you're not having an easy time of it. I can tell."

"If it's about the party, I just had one too many, that was all."

"No, I don't mean just that. You're a troubled man, Wilson."

"I'm doing all right," said Wilson defensively. "I think I can adjust as well as the next man, in time."

"Of course you can. But what you need most of all right now is a friend. Someone you can rely on. Someone you can confide in. Me, for example."

"I appreciate that, Bushbane. But let me put it this way. I've *tried* to confide. For instance, the day after the party I called up this fellow Filter and I began apologizing for my behavior, and he was very polite about it, but he absolutely declined to go into the matter. I mean, I tried to explain that what I'd said on the subject of being a grandfather was merely a kind of mental lapse, do you see, but he pretended that I hadn't said anything of the kind. And then," Wilson continued, "I paid a call on Hamrick. I felt I was bound to, for I'd insulted the man, so to speak, but it was the same story. When I attempted to explain this little mixup about his Harvard degree, he looked like I'd said something embarrassing and he turned red and kept trying to assure me that Harvard hadn't been mentioned at all. Well, of course I realize that men in our position must be discreet and that the past is all over and done with, but frankly, Bushbane, this seems to be carrying things a bit far, don't you agree? You see, if I'm to get on a friendly basis with a man—which I'd like very much to do—I have the feeling that I've got a right to know a little something about him. I mean, just between Hamrick and myself, why couldn't he sort of whisper what school he really went to, eh?"

Bushbane listened to Wilson's recital with increasing gravity. "Look here, Wilson," he said. "I want to say first of all that I absolutely understand your feelings. Absolutely. But you've got to realize that this is a passing phase on your part. You've got to be reasonable." He raised one finger, like a schoolmaster. "You've got to remember that these men have made a tremendous monetary investment in a certain personal service, and they can't abide the idea that this investment may be threatened. Look at it from their point of view. Suppose one of them took it into his head to go running about and making references to the past and asking questions and so forth. I ask you, Wilson, that kind of thing might snowball, and pretty soon the whole damned structure would be in jeopardy. And why? I'll tell you why. Because it all rests on faith and trust. Someone who violates that faith and trust . . . well, he's not playing fair with the others. Don't you see?"

"Well, yes, but—"

"No buts, my friend. Believe me, we all have your best interests in mind," said Bushbane, with obvious sincerity. "We want you to join us heart and soul, we really do. You're one of us, after all. You just have to set yourself to act in good faith, to trust . . . and to accept. And we'll help you, Wilson. We stand ready at any hour of the day or night to help you. Filter and Hamrick and the rest, they're all good loyal fellows, of fine upstanding backgrounds, just your kind of people, Wilson, and as sure as I'm sitting here now, my friend, any one of them would rush to your side at the drop of a hat to give you a boost over a tough moment."

Wilson could not help being touched by Bushbane's words, but he also was somewhat puzzled by their meaning. "What kind of tough moment?"

"Well, in case you feel a sort of urge coming on to look backward, to think about things that—well, that aren't part of the life of Antiochus Wilson. That kind of thing isn't healthy, Wilson, as you'll be the first to admit. You *are* Wilson, you see. You've got a responsibility to yourself to build a new and better past, and you can't very well do that if you keep harking back to something that doesn't bear constructively on that point."

"Yes, I suppose you're right."

"So what I'm saying, Wilson, is that you're bound to have low times. You're bound to feel sort of regressive once in a while. All I want is for you to promise me one thing. When you feel yourself slipping into one of these moods, you just call me up—call up Hamrick, or Filter, or Jolson, for that matter, and we'll run right over to see you."

"And do what?"

Bushbane lighted a cigarette. "Why, we'll do something to take your mind off your troubles. Do you play chess or checkers? Like to zip into town for a girlie show? It doesn't matter what. Whatever it is, we'll do it with you—we'll do it *for* you, and pretty soon, you'll be yourself again, and then in time you'll be free of these urges and you can join us, Wilson, in extending the old helping hand to newcomers. Believe me, my friend, that's just about the biggest satisfaction in life—helping others to find a little happiness," Bushbane declared, his gloomy face alight with fervor. "It took me a long time to realize this fact, Wilson. Why, when I remember how in the old days I used to—" He broke off suddenly as if in embarrassment and gnawed his lip. "I mean to say, well—we stand ready to help you, that's all," he concluded, somewhat lamely. "Can we shake on that, Wilson?"

"Of course," said Wilson, warmly. They clasped hands briefly. "I can't tell you how much your words have meant to me, Bushbane. It's lucky that we bumped into each other out here, as a matter of fact," he added, reaching in his pocket for his wallet with the vague notion of displaying his Denver ticket to Bushbane as a token of his new trust. "Are you expecting to meet someone arriving, by the way?" he inquired conversationally.

"Well, no. I came out with the rest of the committee as soon as John called."

Wilson's hand rested on the wallet but did not withdraw it. "What committee?"

Bushbane grinned disarmingly. "Well, you just told

John you were going to be gone for a few days, without saying where, and so he called us."

"Why?"

"Well . . . . to talk to you, Wilson. We were afraid you might be prepared to so something desperate."

"You mean, you followed me out here?"

"In a sense, yes. Filter and Mayberry and myself. We split up to find you. The reason I dragged you back to this booth," Bushbane added with a conspiratorial wink, "was that I thought I'd do better with you alone. I mean, Filter and Mayberry are fine fellows, but a little on the direct-action side, and they might have offended you."

"I see," said Wilson.

"But everything's all right now, isn't it? That is, you're over your depressed state, aren't you?"

"Absolutely."

"Fine. Look here, Wilson. You're going to forget this nonsense about Las Vegas, aren't you? The thing to do in the first few months, you see, is stay with the gang, and then when you get your sea legs, there's no reason in the world why you can't trust yourself to go anywhere you please and do anything you please, within reason. But going off by your lonesome at this stage—well, that's a bit risky."

"I see your point," said Wilson, shoving his wallet down more firmly into its pocket.

"You know what the saying is about freedom," continued Bushbane persuasively. "Eternal vigilance, Wilson. That's the way freedom grows. Here, I've got an idea. Bob Hamrick and I have planned a little outing to the city for tonight. A good meal, a good show, and then afterward, there's a little place on the hill with Chinese girls. You've got no idea, Wilson, what tricks those Chinese girls can play. We just discovered it last month. How about it—you game?"

Wilson hesitated for just an instant. "Of course," he said. He glanced toward the door with an uneasy expression. "There's just one favor, though, if you wouldn't mind."

"Name it."

"I'm a little—embarrassed by all this, Bushbane. My behavior, I mean."

"Forget it, Wilson."

"And right now I'd rather not face your other two committee members. Do you think you could get them to go on back without seeing me?"

"Sure thing. Look, I'll pick you up at your place about five, okay?"

"Five ought to be just right for me, Bushbane . . ."

By five o'clock, however, Wilson was in a taxicab on his way from the Denver airport to the town nearby where his daughter lived. He had telephoned in advance, naturally, saying that he had been a close friend of her late father, and had received a rather hesitant invitation to come for cocktails.

Now, as the cab drummed over an ice-patched road beside the wall of snowy mountains, Wilson was unpleasantly conscious of his guilt. First of all, by deceiving poor Bushbane, he had violated a deep, instinctive taboo: one simply did not lie to an honest man—and Bushbane was clearly such a man—particularly if one expected to have further dealings with him. He had forfeited Bushbane's trust, and as a matter of fact he would not exactly have improved his standing with the other men, either. There would be long faces and reproving glances when he returned to the colony, that was clear, Wilson thought. But on the other hand, he felt he had the right to decide for himself where he might travel and when, without the intervention of Bushbane and his committee.

"What number was that, sir?" the cabdriver inquired, as he slowed at the outskirts of the town.

"Three twenty-seven."

Sally, his daughter. He felt guilty about her, too. And fearful. Suppose she penetrated his masquerade . . . suppose the eyes and voice and mannerisms gave him away . . . suppose he made some revealing conversational blunder? His hands were cold and damp. He wiped them on his handkerchief, dropped the handkerchief accidentally on the muddy floor of the cab, and, despairing, let it remain there.

Sally greeted him calmly at her door. "Mr. Wilson? Oh, please come in. Let me take your hat . . ."

He had braced himself irrationally against the shock of her recognition. Stupid of him. It undoubtedly only made him look strained and awkward, when he should have appeared genial, friendly, debonair.

"Ah, yes, um." He so feared he would call her Sally that he resolved to call her nothing at all. "And this is your, ah—pleased to meet you, doctor."

His son-in-law was a wiry, dark little man, with a faintly amused and superior expression no doubt copied from some exalted member of the medical school faculty. He frisked Wilson professionally with his eyes, as if his guest were some cadaver laid out to illustrate a surgical problem.

"Bourbon?"

"Yes, thank you." Wilson had dared give Sally no more than a glance at first, for there had been a shock, but perversely he was the one who had failed in recognition. She *was* Sally, wasn't she? She must be. And yet it was only gradually, with occasional furtive looks at her, that he was able to reconstruct in his mind an acceptable image of his daughter. She was not pregnant, but all the same there had been a distinct physical change in the eighteen months since he had seen her. Nothing gross or obvious; still, she was clearly no longer the rather angular and excitable creature whose church wedding had been the triumph of Emily's career. Sally was placid now, formal, composed. The alteration of maturity, perhaps, Wilson thought. He cleared his throat, not knowing what to say, not sure just why he had made this visit. Had he expected to find his little darling toddling about and shrieking "Daddy!" as she saw him ascend the steps? No, the child was gone, so was the energetic virgin, and in their place was a rather aloof young woman who had moved into matronliness. Change and mobility. Thus, life. He swallowed some of the bourbon and forced a smile, conscious that these two young people were waiting for him to justify his visit. Their curiosity was stifling.

"Well!" he began, heartily. "It's a pleasure—"

The cry of a baby in the next room so startled him that his hand shook. Some of the liquor splashed out on his wrist.

"You have a child?"

"Oh, yes. He's two months old now."

"But you never—your father never mentioned that you were going to have one."

"I guess he didn't know. Did he, Sam?" she asked her husband. "Well, anyway, I think he died just about the time we were certain of it—you know, the third month. Would you like to take a look at him?"

"I certainly would."

His grandson was red with fury, kicking puny legs, his pink mouth disproportionately huge, but even so Wilson triumphantly detected his immortality in such tiny matters as the ears, whose lobes hung free, unlike those of the father. He glanced with secret relish from the howling baby to a wall mirror—where he saw an ungrandfatherly Antiochus Wilson transfixed in virile leanness, and noticed, too, that the surgeons had sewn the lobes tight.

"What's his name?"

"He's Sam Junior," said Sally, applying a pacifier to the open mouth.

"Oh. I thought possibly you might have . . ." He shrugged and smiled into his drink. "A fine baby. I'm sure your father would have been—delighted by him. It's a shame he didn't at least know about it, before . . ."

They moved back into the living room.

"Being a grandfather," Wilson remarked, "I mean, it's an experience for a man. Something new. And, well, it sort of demonstrates the continuity of life, doesn't it?" They made no response. He was aware that their curiosity about him had given way to impatience.

"Actually," he went on hastily, trying to improvise an adequate reason for his visit, "your father asked me to drop in on you if I ever passed through Denver, just to extend his—um." He coughed and fumbled in his pocket for cigarettes. "I saw him shortly before his— his death, you see, and he spoke very fondly of you, and it was his greatest wish to come out for a visit."

"He never seemed to be able to break away." Her voice implied indifference, rather than reproach.

"Oh, he wanted to. He wanted to very much," Wilson insisted. "He was terribly attached. It was just that his position required . . . unusual fidelity. He carried heavy responsibilities, your father did."

Sally merely nodded.

"He was a fine man," Wilson declared, shamelessly, determined to inspire some reaction. "Devoted to his family. Why," he added almost defiantly, "there was nothing he wouldn't do for them. I mean, he saw they got the best kind of surroundings, and clothes and things, and a decent environment . . ." He detected a look of boredom on Sally's face. It outraged him. "Why do you suppose he worked so hard to be a success at a job he didn't really like? For his family, that's why. He certainly wasn't doing it for his own amusement." He broke off suddenly, for he sensed that he was on the verge of going too far. They were regarding him quizzically. His son-in-law's eyes seemed to be scanning his face with microscopic intensity, probing for little surgical scars . . . He reached for his handkerchief, not remembering that he had left it on the floor of the cab. Another frustration. He sighed. "Well. I hope his death wasn't too great a blow to your mother."

"She's doing quite well," said Sally.

"Fine, fine. I suppose she's sold the house."

"Oh, no. She's still living there. She wouldn't want to move away from her friends."

"Of course not, no." He forced a smile. His glass was empty; they were making no move to refill it. He supposed he should leave, but he wondered whether the baby would not wake again to be fed or changed. He wanted a chance to study it more closely.

"It's nice to know . . ." His smile ached on his cheeks. Know what? That he wasn't missed? "I'm sure your father would be happy to know, that is," he stammered, and then feeling an imperative need to change the topic, he turned to his son-in-law. "Well, doctor, I imagine you'll be moving into a Denver practice one of these days, eh?"

"As a matter of fact, no. We're established here now."

"Of course. But I mean eventually."

"No, not even eventually." The young man displayed what struck Wilson as a smug little smile. "This town suits us. My office is a block away." He glanced at his wife. "Sally and I have moved around enough in our lives already."

"I lived in six different places by the time I went to college," Sally said absently, looking toward the baby's room.

"Six?" Wilson frowned down at his hands. Surely it hadn't been that many. He began to count on his fingers; then, guiltily, stopped. Their eagerness for his departure was almost palpable. "Six," he repeated. "Yes, that's a lot, naturally. But it's the way people live in this country. Moving around, I mean. Trying to better their lot. You can hardly blame your father for that."

"I'm not blaming him for anything," Sally said coldly. "Sam, perhaps Mr. Wilson would like another drink."

"Oh, no," said Wilson. "I've really got to be going." He shifted position in his chair. "But on the question of social mobility, I think you'll have to admit that it's part of the process of . . . well, of individual freedom. It's what we've been working toward in this country. I mean, people don't have to stay put in one place."

"It might be better if they did," the young man said, with a touch of sharpness.

"Yes, of course. Moving a family is an unsettling business. But it's the price one pays for—for benefits." Wilson wiped his forehead with his hand, once more regretting the loss of his handkerchief. "What I'm trying to say is, this is the way things are in America. People move, that's all. You can't stop it, unless"—he attempted a chuckle—"you're prepared to have a dictatorship."

The son-in-law closed his eyes, as if impatient to the point of hostility. "We have so many authoritarian controls as it is," he muttered, "that another one would hardly be noticed. People oughtn't to be permitted to move, unless they can demonstrate that it's in the interests of society as a whole."

"You're jesting, surely."

"Not completely."

"But, speaking in all seriousness, that sounds a lot like socialism. A man in your position—a physician—can hardly be inclined toward socialism."

The son-in-law blinked wearily at Wilson. "We already have socialism, to a large extent. That's just the trouble. It's socialism without any real controls. Disorganized socialism."

"My husband is actually rather on the conservative side," Sally interjected, as if she were explaining some simple class problem to a backward pupil.

"Freedom," said the young doctor, with the bitterness of a man whose dinner is being delayed by an unwanted visitor. "This freedom you speak of—it's an illusion. Nobody knows how to make use of it. I refer to the great mass of people, naturally. They need to be protected from this freedom, Mr. Wilson, and frankly, if it takes a form of government which involves strict and severe controls, well, I for one will be happy to see the day. Provided," he added, with a wave of one hand, "they leave people like you and me alone."

"Yes, I see what you mean." Wilson was impelled by a powerful desire to leave. He no longer thought of the baby. "Really, I must be going." He rose to his feet, and Sally and her husband stood up with ungraceful readiness as he did so.

"Must you really?" But she was taking his hat and coat from the closet. "There's a cabstand at the corner, unless you'd rather telephone."

"No, please. The corner will be fine." He struggled into his coat. He stared wonderingly into the curved, calm face of what had once been his daughter. "Your father has always been a Republican—a liberal Republican," he mumbled. The baby howled. She glanced behind her, toward the summoning voice. "He's always tried to stay in step," Wilson said anxiously, "with the times. He . . . well, goodbye."

"Goodbye, Mr. Wilson."

The sidewalk was unfamiliar in the darkness. He proceeded cautiously toward the corner, afraid that he might stumble. Behind him the breeze carried the cry of the child.

He returned to the airport, picked up his suitcase, and went to a hotel. He decided not to bother about dinner. Sleep was what he needed most, but no sooner had he tipped the bellboy, flung his coat and hat on a chair, and sunk wearily down on the bed, fully clothed, than the telephone buzzed at him. It was Charley, calling long distance.

"Charley. How the devil did you know where—"

"Never mind that." Charley sounded aggrieved. "See here, old man. I'd like to know what's gotten into you. First we get you all nice and settled down on the Coast and then you go chasing around where you've got no business being. It's not proper, old boy. You're demonstrating a pretty negative approach, if I may say so, and the boys back at the colony are darned cut up about it, too."

"I'm sorry about that," Wilson said, defensively. He loosened his tie with his free hand and sighed. "I thought it wouldn't hurt just to make one quick little visit."

"All right. You've had your little visit. Look," said Charley, obviously struggling to master his peevishness, "let's examine this thing from an ethical standpoint. Is it fair to go rooting around in somebody else's past? I mean, what earthly good does it do? You've got your own life to live. Live it. Let bygones be bygones. All this talk about Harvard and grandchildren—that simply doesn't fit the present situation, old boy. Face up to it. Everybody's better off the way things are—"

"You're absolutely right, of course," said Wilson. He was too tired to protest.

"—and the stakes are important," Charley continued. "Not just for you, but for your friends. They've gone to a great deal of trouble to find their happiness, and now you've got them all worried and bothered, because they feel kind of responsible for you. It's a brotherhood, old boy," he declared, more expansively. "We're all in this thing together. Myself included, you see, because I'm your sponsor, in a manner of speaking. You wouldn't want to let old Charley down, would you?" he inquired in a jesting tone, although Wilson could detect a note of real concern in his voice.

"I'm sorry, Charley. It won't happen again. It was a mistake to come out here, I guess."

"That's more like it."

"But I can't help feeling there's been an injustice done. A real injustice. You remember Sally—what a sweet affectionate kid she was—"

"Don't start on that, old boy."

"No, just let me finish. She doesn't know me, Charley. I don't mean me now, but me—before. It seemed, well, like she sort of wrote me off as some old stupid fuddy-duddy who didn't matter alive or dead, one way or the other."

"Forget it."

"I'm willing to forget it, Charley. I really am. But it's pretty damned upsetting to find out that your own flesh and blood didn't give two hoots about you, when you'd worked and slaved for so many years—"

"Old boy, this is being negative again."

"Just let me talk a minute. That husband of hers, for example. Smug little fascist, that's what he is. One of these little tin medical gods. I tell you, it makes me sick, thinking how the pair of them will be raising that boy of theirs. A grandfather's influence could be decisive, Charley. I realize I'm in no position right now to do anything to that end, but—well, you should have heard the things that fellow said—"

"Look," said Charley, firmly. "You take a sleeping pill and get a good night's rest. I'll get in touch with Bushbane and have him out in Denver by morning."

"I don't need Bushbane. I don't want Bushbane. I'm able to get back under my own steam. The point is, Charley, that a man ought to be able to talk about the things that bother him without being shushed up all the time," said Wilson. "By the way," he went on, tartly, "do you know who Bushbane is married to? Sue. S-u-e, Sue, that's who." There was a considerable silence at the other end of the line. Wilson felt a pang of remorse. "Sorry, Charley," he added. "I didn't mean to stir up old memories."

"Think nothing of it," said Charley, gamely. He puffed out a breath that sounded across the transcontinental wires like the rustling of leaves.

"For all I know," Wilson said, trying to soothe his friend further, "Emily may have remarried by now, too." He was suddenly appalled by the idea. "A rich widow's an easy mark, by God." *His* money. The sense of injustice mounted. "Some slick young gigolo—"

"Old boy," Charley interrupted. His voice was weak with urgency. "In the name of our friendship, I want you to promise me to go back to the Coast. It—it means a lot to me. Believe me, you can't know how much it means to me. We're—we're sort of tied together, you and me."

"I don't understand."

"It doesn't matter. But you will go back, won't you?"

"Well, yes. I said I would."

"And you'll forget all about this other business. Won't you?"

"I'll do my best, Charley."

"Just play the game, that's all," said Charley, unsteadily. "Happiness. It's within our reach, old man. Remember that. And just—play the game . . ." His voice cracked. "Goodbye."

"Goodbye, Charley."

Wilson sat for some time on the edge of the bed, his hands folded in his lap. His thoughts were confused; he could not seem to order them. He was sorry for Charley, of course, although he could not quite see why the mention of Sue's remarriage should be so upsetting. Emily . . . well, that was a different thing, quite different. Emily had been solid and loyal in her way, and certainly faithful; the idea of her as the wife of some stranger impressed him as being most inappropriate. Undignified, in fact. It would be, he felt, quite unlike Emily to do such a thing. The fact that she had not sold the house was encouraging; at least it indicated that she was not one of these giddy creatures who go fluttering down to Miami or Jamaica the moment their spouses are tucked underground. On the other hand, he reflected, she might have found some man right there in Connecticut; perhaps some fellow who'd lost his wife. Someone like Pierce Johnson, with his big calf-eyes and little brush mustache. Johnson's wife had been seriously ill, hadn't she? She might be dead by now, leaving Johnson free to go mooning about other men's wives . . .

He seized the telephone. "Operator? Let me have long distance, please."

"One moment, sir."

His heart was pounding painfully and the receiver seemed terribly heavy in his hand. He had the feeling that he was under the solemn and reproachful observation of Charley, of Bushbane, and of John, and as he glanced guiltily around the room he saw, in the full-length mirror on the closet door, Antiochus Wilson regarding him suspiciously. The lips of the image moved. It whispered: "You fool . . . !"

"Long distance," said the operator cheerfully.

"Ah . . . never mind. I'm sorry. I'll call—later."

He put the receiver down. For several minutes he stared silently at the image in the mirror, waiting for it to move or speak again, but it merely eyed him with sullen audacity, and only when he slumped back on his pillow and swung his legs up on the bed did it vanish.

But still he sensed its presence. It was there in the room with him, slipping stealthily from one mirror to another, watching him. The telephone buzzed. He sat upright. Charley again—or Bushbane, possibly. No, by God, he would not answer. Swiftly he pulled his tie tight, grabbed his coat and hat from the chair, and went out of the room, letting the phone ring on and on behind him.

In the lobby, he hesitated, not knowing what to

do. A family group paced past him on the way to the hotel dining room—a lean young man holding a small boy by the hand, accompanied by a young woman, evidently in the middle stage of pregnancy; and right behind them, a stout gentleman in a well-tailored suit escorting a thin, beaky woman wearing mink and flowers. Three generations celebrating some anniversary, Wilson decided. He could almost smell the odor of long relationships—familiarity, apathy, weariness—that seemed to radiate from them. The child was tired and fussy. The young wife looked slightly nauseated, and the older woman was recounting some complaint to the portly gentleman, whose face displayed a look of disciplined boredom. The man's eyes rested for a moment on Wilson's face, and in that moment Wilson seemed to catch a glimpse of envy, self-pity, and, as the man turned his head away again patiently toward his wife, a mild despair.

"A table for one, sir?"

Wilson stopped short. It seemed that he had trailed along behind the irritable family group right up to the door of the dining room, and the headwaiter was addressing him politely, looking somewhat askance at the coat and hat he still held.

"Um, oh, no." Wilson was confused. "I think I'll eat later on, actually."

"Very good, sir."

He turned away and went hesitantly back through the lobby, where tall mirrors glittered in the brilliance of chandelier light. Everywhere he glanced he seemed to see the image of Antiochus Wilson. He stopped and turned to face it. The figure in the glass had the appearance of reality, of being a living man, and yet was without substance . . . a fleshless apparition, this reflection of himself. He stepped closer to it; obediently, the image advanced to meet him. He wondered whether it would not be possible for him to merge with it finally, so that he might become forever fixed in the coldness of the shining glass, a two-dimensional representation of a man—

He started nervously as he heard his name being cried aloud by a bellboy. He turned hastily away from the mirror. The page-call—that would be Bushbane, growing anxious. Or perhaps Bushbane had telephoned some Denver reborn to seek him out and help him over what Bushbane had called "a tough moment." My God, yes, there would be plenty of reborns to call on; they must be spread over the entire country by now. That tweedy fellow standing at the registration desk—he might be one of them. Bushbane's Denver correspondent, dutifully answering a summons to assist a comrade temporarily in distress. What would the man suggest? A game of chess? Chinese girls?

Wilson hurried out to the street. If he had to converse with someone, he would prefer that plump gentleman who had so gloomily ushered his family into the hotel dining room—the whining grandchild, the bilious daughter, the skinny son-in-law, the irritable wife—all the sour proofs of a life in depth. With such a man, one could at least have the reassurance of an unimpeachable reality.

"Cab, sir?"

"Y-yes, thank you."

He had the impression that the man in tweeds had spotted him and was lumbering in his wake.

He climbed into the taxi. The driver's vicious little face stared at him from the photograph on the licensing permit. The man asked: "Where to?"

"I want to go to—to a night club. I don't know the town. You pick one."

The taxi moved out into the midevening traffic. Wilson glanced through the rear window. He saw no tweedy figure emerge from the hotel, but it mattered little. There were so many of them that he could not hope to elude their kindly pursuit. Indeed, how could Charley have phoned him so soon after he had checked in at the hotel, if he had not been followed and watched every step of the way?

" . . . You want something big with a floor show, mister?"

"Well, yes. That is—no, not exactly. I thought some place a little quieter."

The driver hesitated, estimating his client's intentions. "You sure it's a night club you want, mister?"

"Yes."

"Yeah, well, okay . . ."

The place the driver selected was almost pitch-dark inside. The air was heavily scented with perfume and liquor. In one corner, a man in a blue tuxedo sat playing a piano with an illuminated keyboard; nearby stood a girl apparently nude but wearing flesh-colored tights and tiny stars on her breasts, moving her arms about in imitation of some Oriental dance of gesture, as yellowish and roseate lights alternately passed across her.

Wilson sat at a tiny table and ordered brandy. Gradually his eyes adjusted to the darkness and he perceived the shapes and shadows of the other patrons, spotted with the glowing ends of cigarettes. In time, he was able to identify male and female by their clothing, but their faces remained indistinguishable in the gloom, and he was thankful both for that and for the fact that their conversations were whispered, perhaps out of consideration for the performers. He felt peaceful, and anonymous. The brandy comforted him. He gazed placidly at the girl, and thought that he would be content to remain as he was indefinitely, sipping liquor and watching the awkward and pretentious movements of her arms. She reminded him of Sara Jane, a resemblance that was heightened when he noticed that she seemed to be chewing gum.

A woman sat down at his table. "Do you mind? I'm waiting for someone and it's so crowded—"

"Not at all. Please, um."

He had been caught off guard and had not had time to rise, which slightly annoyed him, for the woman appeared to be a lady, well-dressed and with a pleasant voice.

"Would you let me offer you something while you're waiting?" he asked, anxious to prove his politeness.

"Well, really, it's awfully kind of you, but—"

"A little brandy? It's rather good."

She smiled. Or at least he thought she smiled, for even at close quarters it was difficult to make out the arrangement of another person's features.

"Let me order anyway," he insisted. "You needn't touch it, if you don't want to."

"All right, then. Permission granted."

"Splendid."

A waiter was nearby. Wilson placed his order more loudly than he had intended, and he realized that he was getting drunk. No matter. He turned back to his companion, and, lighting her cigarette, saw with satisfaction that she looked like a decent, cheerful woman. A bit too much rouge for his taste, but perhaps that was the custom in these parts.

"You know, you're the first real person I've had a chance to talk to for a terribly long time," he said earnestly.

"My goodness. That sounds grim. Where are you from?"

"California. A bunch of phonies out there. I mean it," said Wilson, "literally. You know, they take a man at face value out there."

"So I've heard."

"No, you don't understand." He felt a great impulse to unburden himself before Bushbane arrived to lead him away. "There are some people I've come to know who aren't at all what they seem. I mean, they're decent fellows and all that, but they've turned their backs on the past, in a sense. Some of them have changed their names, even," he added, aware that he was not expressing himself as freely as he should, perhaps through the intervention of a subconscious allegiance to Charley and the others.

"Sounds like movie stars," she said.

"No, no. Quite a different thing. Hard to explain." He sat moodily for a moment. The rose and yellow girl had vanished. In her place stood a young man, whispering a song into a microphone. "The point is," said Wilson, "that a man likes to be liked for his inner qualities. That's what I mean. Face value is all very well for the ordinary sort of human experience, but suppose you change the face? Then you lose the value, don't you?"

The woman laughed softly and touched his hand. "You'd better let me have your brandy, too. It's good, but it's not that good."

"No, I'm serious. I mean, it's nice to know you can change your face, but actually going ahead and doing it has certain drawbacks. For example, I'm a grandfather—and at the same time, I'm *not* a grandfather."

"You don't look like a grandfather to me."

"Exactly. Face value." Wilson paused self-consciously and sighed. "You must be wishing your husband would show up so you wouldn't have to listen to any more of my nonsense."

"I'm sure it isn't nonsense. It's just a little complicated. And it isn't my husband, as a matter of fact. I'm a widow."

"Oh, I'm sorry."

"I've gotten quite used to it, really. It's been almost a year. I was lonely at first. Well," she added, with a decisive note in her voice, "I'll tell you something else, too. I've just about come to the conclusion that the person I've been waiting for isn't going to come after all—"

"What a nuisance."

"—and I've been thinking that what you need right now is a good strong cup of coffee. I hope you won't think I'm the kind of woman who goes around picking up strange men in bars, but it occurred to me you might like to see me home. I'll make you some coffee and I'm sure you'll feel much better."

"I'd—I'd like that a lot." But he was confused by the fact that her knees were now touching his, and that she was very gently massaging his hand with her fingers.

"Good. Well, you pay the bill like a good boy, and we'll set off . . ."

In the taxi, they exchanged a long, hearty kiss, and then sat comfortably close in an embrace.

"You're younger than I thought," she said, studying his face.

"I'm older than I look."

"Maybe it's because you have no family responsibilities."

"Maybe." He laughed, and the cab seemed to tilt. "But it's a little strange at first, even when you look in the mirror. It didn't use to be—"

"You've lost your wife," she said keenly, as if she had divined the secret behind his incoherence.

He laughed again. "Yes."

She touched his hand. "It makes things lonely. I know. And almost anything's better than being alone."

"It was very sudden," he added.

"So was mine—my husband. He went on a business trip to New York and died in a hotel. It was a cerebral hemorrhage."

"I beg your pardon?"

"You know—a stroke."

"In a New York hotel—"

"Yes."

Wilson's face bloomed with perspiration.

"What's wrong?" she asked.

"Nothing. I just remembered something. Tell me . . . when did you stop being—lonely?"

"Oh, about four months ago." The taxi pulled over to the curb in front of a large and handsome apartment building. "Here we are," she added, "home." He did not move to open the door. "Well, don't you want to come up?" she asked.

"One thing, excuse me. How often—how many times have you been, um, not lonely?"

"I don't think I quite understand you," she said, coldly.

"I'm sorry. I didn't mean to imply—"

"Look. If you'd rather not have the coffee, you needn't."

"It's not that. I—I just remembered I have a plane connection to make. It must have been the brandy. Completely slipped my mind."

"All right."

He opened the door for her and bowed.

"I'm sorry."

"Never mind," she said. She gazed at him for a moment. "You don't know what it means, being alone," she said in a soft, angry voice. "Not really."

"Oh, yes I do. Really."

But she had turned away and was swiftly walking across the broad pavement toward the glass doors of the apartment building.

Wilson climbed back into the cab.

CHAPTER 5

IT WAS raining in New York; a slow, enveloping rain that seemed to adhere to the sidewalks and streets like a coating of grease. The tops of the buildings faded into mist, but no one looked up. People were hurrying along with their heads lowered beneath hats and swaying umbrellas, dodging puddles and each other, and plunging fatalistically into the paths of buses and taxis.

Wilson stood under the awning of the mid-town hotel where he had registered. Across the street, massive office buildings drew in and expelled their portions of the hastening crowd through mechanically revolving doors; he reflected that inside these buildings, the elevators also were in full operation . . . little steel boxes rushing up and down to eject loads of figures at various levels, and to suck in others.

He shivered, involuntarily, and glanced behind him. He had been followed, surely; even now, he supposed, he was under observation. That athletic-looking gentleman who stood just inside the lobby peering out as if waiting for a break in the rain—he could be one of them . . . or the tall man in a trench coat with a rolled-up newspaper stuck under one arm like a swagger stick who had come out of the hotel and was standing nearby, but who had declined the doorman's offer to hail a taxi. Indeed, both men might be members of the brotherhood—and others could be advancing, too, to surround him, to take him gently away so that he would be prevented from indulging in any further acts of foolishness.

The tall man turned tentatively toward him, apparently about to speak. Wilson stepped to the edge of the awning, letting the street crowd bump around him; but he went no farther, for it occurred to him, perhaps illogically, that if he went into the street and across, he might be pulled into the mechanically revolving doors of the opposite buildings and be lost inside forever. One of those doors—any one—might be the entrance to the company's headquarters, and from the rain-slick windows far above the patient clerks in their tan jackets might be staring sadly down. The hotel behind him—for all he knew it could be the one where the cadaver facsimile of himself had been discovered on a summer evening nine months ago . . . He felt uncomfortably close to unpleasant discoveries.

The tall man touched his sleeve. "Excuse me—"

"Sorry." Wilson turned to one side and hastened off with the moving crowd. He was not ready for them yet.

He needed time to think. The rain annoyed him; he ducked his head angrily and tipped his hatbrim down. Let the tall man follow him. Let them all follow him. A hundred of them could not keep him from doing what he had to do to salve his sense of injustice. It was not the company's fault, of course. The company had nothing to do with it. It was his own private, personal affair, and the company would simply have to be patient with him until he had concluded it to his satisfaction.

He turned into a drugstore, and stood breathing harshly for a moment among stacks of plastic toys and gadgets that all but obscured the soda fountain counter and the telephone booth at its far end. A row of balloons with painted grinning faces confronted him. Behind them, ping-pong balls trembled in the air, supported by invisible fingers of air, and little mechanical men shuffled jerkily to and fro on a magnetic board.

He reached the telephone booth with the tall man at his heels.

"You're Wilson, aren't you?"

Wilson turned and answered bitterly: "I'm not really sure." But the tall man seemed so inoffensively troubled and uncertain, that his anger dwindled. "Look here," he added, "I know you mean well, but this isn't exactly your affair. It's mine." He stepped into the booth and pulled out a handful of change.

The tall man eyed him ruefully. "Don't do it, Wilson," he said.

"Do what?"

"You know." The tall man made a despairing gesture with his hands. "We've all been through the mill, Wilson. Believe me. It won't do any good." Wilson jiggled the door handle impatiently. "I mean," the man went on, "haven't you had enough of it already?"

"That's my business. It doesn't affect the company."

"No, I mean for you. It's wrong for you, Wilson."

"I'm afraid I'll have to be the judge of that."

"Wilson, you'll be sorry—"

Wilson slid the door shut. The tall man hovered nearby for a moment and then, as he saw Wilson push a coin into the box, he backed off reproachfully and became lost to sight among the balloons.

The sound of Emily's voice so startled Wilson that he almost forgot to wrap the mouthpiece with his handkerchief, to disguise his own.

"Ah, Mrs.—um . . ." He could not bring himself to pronounce the name. And it might no longer be the one she used. The booth was stifling. He coughed.

"Yes?"

"Excuse me. My name is Tony Wilson. You don't know me, I'm afraid, but I was a fairly good friend of your late husband's, and—well, he often told me whenever I was East I ought to call him up, and, ah . . ."

"Yes?"

"Of course that was last year, before he, ahem." Wilson laughed, inappropriately. "But I didn't want to let the occasion pass without conveying my deepest personal. My sympathies. Those of us who." He coughed again and glanced out guiltily. A woman was waiting for him to finish. Behind her he noticed the tall man's hat seemingly perched atop one of the grinning balloons.

"Yes, it was a great loss," Emily said formally. "It's very thoughtful of you to call."

"Well, I was anxious to extend my—that is, I wonder if it would be possible for me to. I'd like very much," said Wilson, wiping his brow with the free end of his handkerchief, "to pay a call, if it's convenient."

"Yes, I see. Well—"

"Your late husband was a man of many facets," he went on quickly, aware of her hesitation. "He was . . . well, it's impossible to talk about it over the phone, but of course naturally I have no intention, no wish of stirring up your, um, grief. I'm here just today and tonight before I go back West, and if it's not convenient, then of course, naturally—"

"Not at all." She made the little clucking sound that meant she was thinking. He shut his eyes. He could well imagine her blinking her lids rapidly, pouting out her cheeks, poised there by the telephone stand in the foyer, considering what to do. "It's terribly kind of you, Mr. Wilson. I'm having a few people in for cocktails at five o'clock, as it happens, but if you'd care to drop in then . . ."

"You're sure it would be all right?"

"Oh, positively."

"I'd only stay for a few minutes," he went on, anxious to soothe away her obvious reluctance. Emily's parties were always so precisely planned. He realized how dismayed she might be at the prospect of having a stranger appear to upset the social balance. He fumbled for a further justification. "I'm a painter, Mrs.—um. An artist. Actually, I always admired your late husband's watercolors."

"Really?"

"Not that he was a professional. But he did have . . . something. And, well, I wondered if maybe as a kind of token I might pick out one of his pictures from the walnut cupboard in the garage." He coughed once more, hoping to cover what would appear to be a strange familiarity with the furnishing of a garage which he would not have had the opportunity of seeing.

"Oh. Well, as a matter of fact, the garage has been cleaned out."

"You threw them away?"

"Not exactly. But anyway," she said quickly, "if you'll come at five, I'm sure I can find something as a remembrance. Do you have the address?"

"Yes . . ."

He replaced the receiver. Of course she would have chucked out his watercolors. Why not?

He wandered out again to the street. The tall man was waiting there in the rain, humbly allowing himself to be buffeted by the crowd.

Wilson went up to him. An umbrella bobbed between them and passed on, its silver tip glistening.

"What do you want me to do?"

The tall man looked silently down at him for a moment. He seemed ill at ease; the rain was slanting into his face, but he made no attempt to shield himself from it.

"Go back to California," he said, finally.

"I will, tomorrow."

"You ought to go now, Wilson. Let me go with you—out to the airport."

Wilson shook his head. "I'm sorry."

The tall man sighed. He appeared on the verge of repeating his request, but then apparently thought better of it, and merely waved his hands clumsily in a gesture of resignation.

"What difference does it make—today or tomorrow?" Wilson asked. "Look, I'm not going to do anything stupid, you know. I just want—well, I want to check up on a few matters. You people didn't really give me time to make the proper preparation when I was processed. I had no idea I would be required to drop everything all at once. That's hardly a businesslike way of handling one's affairs," he went on determinedly. "I thought surely I'd have a day or two to complete my arrangements."

"Like what?" The tall man spoke softly, as if the question was of no consequence.

"Well, I don't think the details are important. It's a matter of principle." A sagging awning loosed a spout of water onto his hat. He dodged aside, too late. "Frankly," he continued, tilting his head to let the water drain from the crown, "I'm not too well pleased with the way the company has dealt with my case. They've made a few mistakes, which they've as much as admitted, and now when all I'm trying to do is smooth out some of the rough edges, they have me followed all over the country like some criminal . . . Are you a company staff man, by the way, or are you—like me?"

"Does it matter?"

"I happen to think it does."

The tall man stared intently at Wilson. He shook his head slowly. "Has it ever mattered? I don't mean with me or you now, but . . . well, ever. In your experience. With your father, maybe, but what I'm trying to say . . ." He waved his hands again, hopelessly. "Just go back . . . to California. I can't explain it."

"What's my father got to do with it?" Wilson asked, but the tall man simply made one final flapping movement with his hands, turned, and walked awkwardly away in the rain, without saying goodbye. Wilson pursued him, ducking away from umbrellas and the ends of awnings.

"Look here. Wait a minute." He tugged at the man's sleeve. "I don't get what you said about my father."

"Oh, I don't really mean your father. I mean, in your father's time, or maybe earlier than that even."

"But that still doesn't make sense."

"I told you I couldn't explain it." The tall man screwed up his features painfully, as if trying to muster the right words. "I mean, what difference does it make to people like you and me? If a man stays on the surface of things all his life, then it's the surface that counts, isn't it? There isn't really anything important but the surface. That's what I'm trying to say. And—

well, here's my surface." He grinned in a forced way and drew one hand down slowly across his face, then thoughtfully examined his fingers. "See? That's all there is—because that's all there ever . . ." He shrugged his shoulders and began walking again.

Wilson kept pace with him. "I think I see what you're driving at," he said soothingly, for he was anxious to prolong the conversation and find out more about the tall man. "But it seems to me you're taking a pretty grim view of things. Take the inner life, for example." He stepped aside to avoid being bumped by a careless trucker's dolly. "Everybody's got an inner life," Wilson persisted, hastening to catch up again. "And things like love and happiness. You can't simply dismiss all of that, my friend."

The tall man did not look at him. "I don't dismiss them."

"Well, dammit. These things don't show. They don't appear on that surface of yours. They're down underneath, inside. That's where they are."

"Why?"

"They've got to be, that's all."

"But if they are, then why did you do what you did?" The man still would not look at him. They stood at a crossing, waiting for the light to change.

"Well, nobody's situation is ideal, and a man has a right to try for improvement," said Wilson, realizing that he was in the ironical position of justifying the company's point of view to someone who had obviously been dispatched on behalf of the company. "Believe me, I have no regrets. No substantial regrets," he amended, but as he spoke the tall man darted out through the traffic with surprising agility, and climbed into a taxicab which had just discharged a fare. "Look here!" Wilson cried out after him, but in vain. The cab pulled away, turned the corner, and was gone.

Wilson stood irresolutely at the curb for a moment, aware of the trickling of rain down the back of his coat collar, the heedless elbows of the crowd, and the grey sweep of traffic; all was in motion, except himself. The sidewalk he stood on trembled as a subway passed beneath it, the traffic signals clicked and whirred—even the massed buildings seemed busy with the noisy processes of mechanical life. Once more he was impressed by their power. It was all automatic—the revolving doors of the entryways, turning constantly at an even rate, and the elevators, which rose and descended without human operators. Some of the offices, too, he reflected, would be equipped with machines that opened doors, and that typed messages—and even perhaps some that responded to inquiries, and announced the quitting hour. He wondered idly what would happen if the machinery got out of hand and began to speed up. The revolving doors, say. If they started whirling, would those who happened to be caught in them be imprisoned and spun dizzily about, or would the centrifugal force fling them out and, by some terrific vacuum, pump in others from the street . . . possibly persons who had no intention of entering that particular building at all, but who would find themselves thrown inside, and then drawn irresistibly into an automatic elevator to be hurled up twenty stories and spat out into a strange office where a mechanical receptionist would seize their hats and coats in its steel claws—?

Someone bumped him hard from behind. He turned, but the transgressor had passed on. He tipped his hat humbly, nevertheless, and said, to no one in particular: "Sorry."

He almost expected to find Emily at the station to meet his train. There were some wives parked in idling cars waiting for their husbands (not many, it was true, for this was an early train), but as Wilson strolled among the homebound commuters, he recalled that Emily would not have been there in any case, for in recent years he had used the grey sedan to get to the station.

He glanced involuntarily toward the parking lot. The car—it was still there, its identity proclaimed by the badge of rust on the right rear fender and the crumpled edge of the bumper where he had struck a telephone pole once, backing up. Emily had not come to meet him . . . but the sedan was waiting right where he had left it on that summer day, as if he had gone nowhere, as if nothing had happened . . . and perhaps if he went over to claim it, climbed in behind the wheel as usual, and drove on home—

"Pardon me."

He leaped back, startled by the voice. A thin, elderly man reached past him for the door handle.

"I-I'm sorry. I—"

"Not at all."

The man slipped inside, glanced at his watch, and jammed a key into the ignition.

Wilson stepped aside, confused, anxious to explain. "I didn't mean to be—to be—"

"Be glad to give you a lift, except—" The man's voice was overridden by the racket of the engine, and the clash of the gears as he shifted into reverse and backed out to swing around and head for the parking lot exit.

Wilson drew his hand from his pocket, where it had been fumbling for his old car keys; he pulled out, instead, his Denver hotel room-key, and at the same time he caught a blurred glimpse of Antiochus Wilson grinning in reflection from the window of the grey sedan as it passed by.

He set his shoulders and started back toward the station. She had sold it. One car was all she needed, to be sure. Even so, he was annoyed that he had not been given the opportunity to dispose of the car himself, for it had been, after all, not an item of family property but rather a personal belonging used only by him, like his cuff links.

He dropped the room-key into the mailbox and telephoned for a taxi.

Waiting for it, he became possessed by the idea that Emily would immediately recognize him—not so much by his voice or his eyes or gestures, the things which the company had been unable to alter, but by the indefinable and possibly even extra-sensory knowledge of his presence, which a wife was bound to have after a quarter-century of marriage. Intuition: the surgeons could not have protected him against that. With Sally there had been no real test, for daughters are accustomed to judge their fathers in terms of superficial external things, but a wife—! How embarrassed Emily will be, he thought. How flustered and confused. To see a stranger suddenly as her husband, the former source of all the binding intimacies of love, of money, of tolerance and coldness, breakfasts and garden planning . . . it would drive her mad. Well, not mad, exactly. Emily was not the kind of person to be driven mad, he reflected. She would consult not a psychiatrist but a lawyer, if indeed she decided that she required any assistance to deal with what she would instantly define as a Social Situation, the resolution of which must be deferred at least until her party was over. And then, he wondered, when they were alone together again, what would she do? Fall on her knees before him to beg him to come back, whatever his changed name and face might be . . . or wait, with suppressed consternation, for him to make the first move? Somehow, he could not quite imagine Emily on her knees, and as for his making the first move, or a move of any kind—

His taxi had arrived. The driver was honking. Wilson hurried to it.

Would she scream, he wondered? Faint . . . slam the door on him . . . or fix him with a look of warning while meaningfully introducing her fiancé—or new husband?

Too late to turn back. He croaked out his address, then sank back sweating against the seat, his eyes closed to shut out the sight of streets and houses which seemed, at this moment, only too grossly familiar.

The taxi stopped; he spilled a handful of change on the floor in back. "Never mind." He thrust a bill at the driver and got out, stumbled on the curb, and only with great difficulty kept from flopping to his knees. "I'm all right," he said, and plunged ahead toward the front door of his house, over the flagstones whose precise positioning he himself had supervised a dozen years before.

He rang.

"Mr. Wilson?"

"Ah, yes—"

The maid who answered was a woman he had never seen before. For a moment he was possessed by the idea that she was Emily, transformed, but then he saw his wife behind her in the foyer. He shuffled forward.

"Mr. Wilson—please come in. I'm so glad you were able to come, after all."

"Thank you."

He waited for the accusation in her eyes, waited for her to gasp and puff; stood there dumbly fingering his hat until the maid finally took it from him, as he stared at Emily with pleading to get it over with, his lips ready with a phrase: *Yes—it's me.*

But she merely smiled and gestured toward his coat. "If you'll—"

"Oh, my coat." He struggled out of it. From the living room came the sound of voices, male and female, slightly subdued in expectation of another guest. He let the maid take the coat, conscious that Emily was regarding him oddly but without surprise, as if he were no more than an eccentric stranger.

He could not bear waiting for recognition. It was intolerable for her to treat him so aloofly. "You have a lovely place, Mrs.—um. I almost feel as though I've been here before. Why," he added, gazing around the foyer, where the sturdy grey walls he remembered had been made remote and brilliant with white, "you've redecorated."

Still no reaction. Only the fixed little hostess smile on the plump unaging face.

"Thank you, Mr. Wilson. Shall we—?"

"Of course." He followed her humbly, out of place. Had she missed the cues—or ignored them?

As they entered the living room, he looked about swiftly, searching for familiar objects, but everything was altered there, too, or gone: some chairs missing, others disguised in new upholstery; the old bookcase vanished, and hanging in its place a gigantic Chinese scroll painting. The solid brown draperies, too, had given way to some light fleecy stuff that billowed saucily in the window-drafts, and where his stout curved reading chair had been there now perched two little flimsy wooden affairs that would split if a man sat down hard on them.

He was only hazily aware of meeting the other

guests. There were two men and two women, none of whom he knew, and he failed to get their names.

"Antiochus Wilson—the painter? Why, I've seen your work. Didn't you do that magnificent seascape with the people upside down?"

It was an eager woman in purple, wearing a pince-nez.

"No, I don't believe—well, yes, actually, I suppose you mean—"

"You called it 'Marine Lights'—that was the title. Oh, and I remember you did the sun green, the way it would look to a fish." The woman pressed insistently at him. "You *did* mean to show how it would look to a fish, didn't you?"

"Quite right, yes. A fish."

The mantel had held his father's Victorian pipe-rack, an octagonal castle of pipes; it, too, was gone. He glanced toward the French doors and saw dimly through the shivering veil of curtains a strange garden, spotted with new shrubs and little brick paths. The roses had been moved, it seemed.

"Excuse me, but the symbolism of the fish," the woman went on, edging around to command his line of sight, "it was so—so right, somehow."

"Thank you."

"So—deliciously ironic. I mean, *lurking* beneath the surface"—she giggled—"in contrast to the mannered—I mean *deliberately* mannered, of course—the mannered innocence of the swimmers."

He smiled and backed stealthily in the direction of the study, his old retreat.

"I teach art," the woman purred, keeping pace.

"I'm sure you do."

He caught a glance of satisfaction from Emily across the room. With her customary adroitness, she had neutralized him with this creature; eccentric or not, husband or not, he had been disarmed and would cause no trouble.

"And I paint a bit myself."

"I see." He sipped his drink and with his free hand casually turned the knob of the study door.

"I'm on exhibition now—"

"Really."

"—in a show. A one-man show." The purple woman smiled and pressed her flat bosom modestly.

"Wonderful."

He glanced inside the study. It wasn't there. Desk, chair, hearth, all gone. Even the walls. She had had them knocked out to enlarge the dining room. He turned accusingly toward his wife. She had no right to do that; to change things around, perhaps, but not to destroy, not to obliterate.

Emily saw him coming and stepped forward calmly, in full command. He stared at her, then lowered his eyes. If she knew, then she did not care; but probably, he thought, she did not know—nor would have known a year ago if, as his former self, he had come home in someone else's suit with his face disguised, say, only by a paste-on mustache.

All he said was, lamely: "Your dining room is . . . very nice."

"Thank you, Mr. Wilson." She was exactly, precisely the same. Everything else was changed, done over, replaced, and different—even her friends had been disposed of, in favor of these strangers—but she was without a mark.

She moved a step closer. "You said you wanted a memento, I think."

"Ah, well—"

Her attitude politely expressed: You have come. Now you may go.

He remembered how she had phrased the invitation over the telephone: " . . . *but if you'd care to drop in.*" The "but" had clearly meant: Don't come. He had ignored it, very well. But now it was time for him to leave, before the politeness chilled.

"I have something. Here." She had maneuvered him into the foyer. She stooped and from behind the closet door picked up a package about the size of a liquor bottle, neatly wrapped. "It isn't a painting, I'm afraid, but—"

"Thank you."

"—it's all I have."

"Of course." Of course, of course, he thought, staring at the package. It was a miracle that even this last small remnant of himself had survived, and perhaps if he had been delayed a day or two, it, too, would have been cast away.

There were voices, his and hers, reciting the formula of goodbye. He was at the door, clutching his coat and hat and package.

"Your late husband," he began, but it was pointless. She would hear nothing; nor, ultimately, did he really wish to speak. Everything that might have been said had either not been said or said and forgotten long ago, and there remained only her good breeding and his despair.

"Goodbye."

"Goodbye, Mr. Wilson."

He turned; behind him, the door clicked. He moved heavily over the flagstones, his hands absently feeling the contours of the package. It was urn-shaped. Halfway to the street, he stopped and tore at the wrapping. Having disposed of everything else, had she now given him the only thing that would be left—the literal remains of the departed banker (or rather those of the cadaver that had taken his place)—the ashes?

But it was only a cup, a tennis trophy awarded to him in his final year at prep school; he had won no others. One word stood out: "Champion."

He remembered that he had neglected to telephone for a taxicab, but there was a car idling at the curb, a strange man sitting behind the wheel, and another, whom he recognized, standing outside holding the door open for him.

"Hello, Bushbane," Wilson said humbly, getting in.

CHAPTER 6

He had no heart to speak. He sat quietly beside Bushbane, holding the tennis cup in his hands, while the
limousine moved powerfully along the streets of the
town, drawing in through its windows the odor of
spring. The yards of the houses were fat with flowering bushes and heavy-headed blooms; the air had the
laboratory sweetness of gasoline. It made him drowsy.

"I'm sorry, Wilson," Bushbane said, finally.

"It doesn't matter."

"No, I suppose not."

It was the hour of return for the commuters from
the city. Men in dark suits with briefcases, their ties
loosened, their hats tipped back, were climbing out of
cars. Some of the earlier arrivals had already changed
into sports clothes and were wandering about in the
gardens with their wives, snipping at the flowers,
squirting poisons here and there with little spray guns.

Wilson recalled that late in the evenings the fogging machines would make their rounds, spraying, too.

"They're killing the bugs," he explained.

"Eh?"

"The bugs. They're spraying all the time, to keep the bugs off. They've been doing that for years and years. I did it, too, Emily and I. We sprayed the garden."

Bushbane gave him a stealthy glance.

"My point is," Wilson continued, absently toying with his tennis trophy, "that the bugs are mostly gone now, but they keep on spraying out of habit. No bugs, Bushbane. The program is a tremendous success. No birds, either," he added, anxious to present a complete picture of his observations, "because the birds lived off the bugs, you see, and now the birds have had to go elsewhere for a living."

"Yes. Well, I never did much gardening myself."

"If you spray long enough—if everybody sprays long enough—I mean, if it's a community project to do a thoroughgoing job of spraying . . . well, you're bound to get rid of the bugs, Bushbane. And if that means losing the birds—well, you can't get something for nothing. I think that's what I'm trying to get across."

"Quite right," muttered Bushbane.

"And the flowers," Wilson went on. "They're flowers that couldn't possibly have been raised when I was a boy. Gigantic. Perfect. Look at those roses in that yard, Bushbane. Roses like that simply didn't exist years ago, except perhaps in a hothouse, under controlled conditions. And now, everybody can have them . . . all you do is feed and spray, feed and spray. Only, as I say, the funny part is that most of the bugs were wiped out years ago, but still people go on spraying. I wonder, suppose they left off spraying for a while, would the old roses come back, do you think?"

Bushbane cleared his throat. "Well—"

"The species would be different, I guess. They'd have to be," said Wilson, thoughtfully.

"Wilson, I can well understand how you've been subjected to a strain—"

"And the bugs would be different, too. Not that it would matter much, because it occurs to me that the bugs no longer have any useful function, in the sense of cross-fertilization, at least in some of the newer varieties of flowers . . ." He yawned enormously, and noticed that the limousine now had turned onto the superhighway, where it was cruising along at tremendous speed toward the setting sun.

"We're going to the airport, I suppose," he asked, sleepily.

"Actually," said Bushbane, "there's a stop we need to make in town."

Wilson nodded and closed his eyes. "Oh, it doesn't matter about my clothes at the hotel. Don't stop on my account, Bushbane." There was no response. "I'm afraid," he added, yawning again, "that I've put you to an enormous amount of trouble."

"Not at all. You just relax. Yes, take a little nap, Wilson. It'll make you feel like a new man . . ." Wilson obediently permitted himself to fall into a deep slumber. Bushbane's comforting phrase seemed to stretch out luxuriously before him, echoing a friendly reassurance. " . . . *a new man* . . ."

He felt the trophy slip from his fingers; he let it fall. The steady hum of the limousine was soothing, for it reminded him that he was being borne along by a masterful and beneficent force to whatever destination had been selected for him by those who, even more than himself, had his best interests at heart; and Bushbane, too—who had been rushed out to be by his side at the crucial moment—Bushbane was still further evidence of the company's deep, almost ardent concern for his welfare. He felt an answering surge of emotion; he wanted to raise his head, to open his eyes, to express to Bushbane not only his apologies for his heedless behavior, but his thankfulness for his good fortune in having friends, in being loved, in having been forgiven, so to speak, the virtually unforgivable sin he had committed. That funny little old man, the company president—hadn't he made it clear at the very beginning that a client could never go back? And yet *he* had gone back, or rather, had tried to go back, and despite this transgression he was being treated with the utmost consideration. He sought to speak, but his drowsiness was too strong; he managed merely to shed a single tear, which lay glistening on his cheek as he slept.

When the limousine stopped at last and its engine was shut off, Wilson was not much surprised on awaking to discover that the car was in an alley, dim and anonymous in the growing dusk of evening.

"Um—" Bushbane began.

"It's all right, really. Of course." Wilson shook himself once and rubbed his face, then climbed readily out of the car before Bushbane was required to urge him. The limousine driver stood respectfully nearby; Wilson smiled at him reassuringly. "Just tell me where I should go," he declared cheerfully, and in fact he did feel remarkably at ease and without the slightest apprehension.

A door in the wall of masonry opened. A uniformed attendant stepped out and said: "This way, Mr. Wilson, if you please."

Bushbane remained in the car; the driver shut the rear door and got in behind the wheel again.

"You're not coming, Bushbane?" Wilson asked, as the engine shook itself to life. "No? Well, of course, naturally I understand . . ." He took a step toward the man who held the building door open for him, to demonstrate his obedience, and turned to wave to Bushbane as the limousine edged forward. "I quite understand, Bushbane. Please convey my kindest regards to Hamrick and the others . . ."

The car's exhaust coughed at him. Bushbane, drawn slowly by, peered out with what seemed to be an embarrassed expression, and tentatively moved his hand in a wave of farewell. "My kindest regards," Wilson repeated, and with as much confidence as if he himself had planned the episode down to the last detail, he turned away from the retreating car and strode toward the open door, realizing that it was not only inevitable but also highly logical and proper that he had been deposited at this particular place, even though he was not certain what would follow.

"Just tell me what to do," he advised the attendant, as they proceeded along a passageway. "Believe me," he added, almost humorously, "I've had my fill of causing you people difficulties. I'll be careful to avoid that kind of thing in the future, I assure you!"

The attendant smiled politely but said nothing. At the end of the passageway he ushered Wilson into a small elevator, closed the door, and pressed an unnumbered button.

"I came in a different way last year," Wilson remarked, as the elevator rose. "But I suppose there's more than one entrance. This is the company headquarters, isn't it?" The attendant made no reply. "Excuse me for asking obvious questions," Wilson went on, hastily. "I realize it's not part of your job to answer things like that. I mean, you're not exactly one of these guided-tour people they have in museums and public buildings—!" He laughed, by way of further apology, but in the close confinement of the elevator cage the laugh had no resonance and sounded choked. The attendant smiled down gravely at his shoes.

"But then I imagine you're accustomed to people like me—taking them up in this elevator, I mean— and hearing them babble on in a silly kind of way," Wilson remarked, anxious to cover the odd sound of that laugh of his, which, he thought, must have been unpleasant for the attendant to hear. "That is, people who talk more than they should . . . indiscreet people. And the strange thing is, as a matter of fact," he continued, somehow unable to keep himself from rambling on, "that all my life—well, my former life, if you know what I mean—all my life, as I say, I've been trained to be discreet. Meaning, among other things, not to talk too much, and to be very careful about what is said even then . . ."

He paused for breath. Either the elevator was an extremely old and slow-moving one, he thought, or else the building was enormously high, for it seemed that they had been rising for several minutes. ". . . and then when I was given my present status, this habit of discretion failed me completely, for some reason," he added, "and—well, frankly, I did things that normally a prudent man would never have done—"

The elevator stopped. The attendant opened the door and politely motioned Wilson forward into a dimly lighted corridor. At the far end, a door stood open, as if waiting for him.

". . . yes, I was quite surprised at times by the way I acted," Wilson continued. "But naturally I realize that all of that business is behind me now, and in all honesty, I can say that I'm not in the least bit sorry—"

"If you'll go down that way, Mr. Wilson," the attendant interrupted mildly, indicating the door at the end of the corridor.

"Eh? Oh yes, of course. Absolutely." Wilson set off

at once along the polished floor, anxious neither to cause by his tardiness even the tiniest disruption in the well-ordered affairs of the company, nor to delay the commencement of whatever corrective measures had been planned to set him straight once again, for he was well aware that his second appearance at the company headquarters could have no other object.

At the doorway he paused. There was a woman in white seated behind a desk in the room, examining some papers in a file.

"I'm Wilson," he said; at the same time she glanced up at him, and he saw that she was the woman who had visited him on the morning of his operation, and with whom he had been so unexpectedly on intimate terms. He was disconcerted by the recollection, not on grounds of morality, but rather because she reminded him afresh how deeply he had violated the trust which the company had placed in him, for now in retrospect it seemed to him that his physical union with her had symbolized the company's desire to do all that it could to prepare him for the great opportunity it was offering.

But she did not seem to recognize him. "Oh, yes, Mr. Wilson," she said, with a friendly but impersonal smile. "Won't you please sit here, sir?"

Wilson sat dutifully, and when she indicated that he was to take a pill that rested on a plate on the desk, he lost no time in gulping it down.

"You, um, probably don't remember me," he began, feeling that he should make it clear that he, at least, recalled their former close association, for it seemed unfair for him simply to sit there in sole possession of such a delicate memory. Then he caught himself abruptly. "Of course. That was when—" He laughed, in embarrassment. "I mean, I was different then."

She smiled, professionally. "Yes, I suppose so," she said. "And then, there are so many gentlemen, you know, and twice as many faces, actually, meaning Before and After, you know, so you hardly get to know someone and then they've gone off, Mr. Wilson."

"Yes, I'm sure that's right."

In the background he could hear a man's voice, muffled by an intervening door, speaking indistinguishable words in a sharp tone.

"That pill is a quick worker, Mr. Wilson," the woman remarked. "Perhaps you'd better lie down now and get good and comfy. There's a cot right over there, if you don't mind."

"Oh, yes." The cot was in the corner; he had not noticed it when he entered. He saw that it was on wheels. "Should I take my shoes off, do you think?"

"It doesn't matter."

He sat on the cot, indecisively wondering whether he should remove his shoes, and then he thought he would not bother. "Well." He cleared his throat and stretched himself out on the cot. "I don't suppose you'd be able to tell me—"

"Just don't you worry about anything, Mr. Wilson." She came over to him and patted his forehead. "Everything's going to work out for the best, sir. You just relax there and be comfortable."

"Thank you." He did feel comfortable. His limbs were beginning to float a little, and he was hardly conscious of lying on anything at all. The woman's hand on his forehead was cool and light, and everything was growing remote, with the exception of the man's voice, which appeared to be much closer now, as if the man had entered the room.

He heard the woman speak, but could not make out her words. With a great effort, he opened his eyes in order to make some response, and saw not her face above him but that of the man. It was familiar, too; it was scarred, unforgettably scarred.

It was the resident physician gazing down at him, and smiling, but not too pleasantly. "Well, so it's Wilson," he said. "I thought you might be back. That's what I thought at the time, and I'm not often wrong . . ." He chuckled, as if Wilson's return were some private joke, and then bending closer, so that Wilson could see each rude discolored segment of his disfigurement, he added: "Yes, sir, Wilson. I did indeed by God think you'd be back—and here you are!" He tilted back his head as if to laugh, but Wilson heard nor saw no more.

His first waking thought some hours later was a startling one, and yet it seemed logical: namely, that he had been restored, surgically, to what he once was. He sat up on the cot and pressed his hands to his face. No bandages. But of course, he reflected, there had been no time for anything so involved as a new series of operations, for clearly he had been put to sleep just for the night.

Morning sunlight was filtering through a single small-paned window high above his head. He glanced up at it, then around the tiny room which was barely large enough to contain the cot, a small bureau, and a wooden chair on which some clothing was folded. He himself was naked, and hungry as well.

An aroma of coffee and bacon originating from beyond the closed door brought him eagerly to his feet, and he began putting on the clothing which had been laid out for him: grey slacks, soft white shirt, wool socks, and bedroom slippers. The slippers gave substance to his impression that he was indeed possessed of the status of a pre-operative patient, who was bound to be given the very best of care pending arrangements for his entry into surgery. He did not actually look forward to the prospect of spending weeks of a frequently painful convalescence, but he was prepared—fully prepared—to endure it, if that was what the company had planned for him.

The likelihood of such a solution became more and more apparent to him with each passing moment. After all, the company had flatly guaranteed his successful rebirth as Antiochus Wilson, and although it was certainly not to blame for the failure of that experiment—despite its occasional miscalculations—nevertheless the obligation remained outstanding. The company owed him a satisfactory rebirth, if not as Wilson, then as someone else. But not as his former self. No, he saw that a true restoration would be out of the question, for the banker was legally dead, and even the company's agile Documents Division, for all of its experience in the fabrication of papers, could hardly be expected to effect a resurrection.

Perhaps, he reflected as he put on a light tan jacket to complete his ensemble, the new identity would combine the best features of the two preceding ones. In any case, he concluded sensibly, the first order of business was breakfast.

The door to his room opened onto a long passageway. He proceeded along it in the direction of the enticing odor of coffee, noticing as he went that many similar cubicles were on either side of the corridor, and although he saw no occupants, he assumed that he thus was but one of a group of clients who, like himself, had found it necessary to return to the company for reorientation.

Opening a door at the end of the corridor, he entered a room that was familiar. It was, in fact, the huge area he had wandered into on his first visit to the company, when he was attempting to find a way out of the building, and he now saw there approximately what he had witnessed before—a considerable number of middle-aged gentlemen seated at desks or in easy chairs, engaged in a variety of pastimes and amusements, each of them wearing a tan cloth jacket similar to the one he had put on. And again, as before, no one seemed particularly to notice his appearance.

Wilson cleared his throat and stepped tentatively forward. One of the men nearby finally glanced at him, and with an indifferent expression indicated an empty desk, on which had been placed a tray bearing a plate of bacon and toast, and a pot of coffee. "I imagine that's yours," the man remarked, neither pleasantly nor otherwise, and lowered his head again to resume his occupation, the examination of a coin collection.

Not exactly a hearty welcome to a fellow patient, Wilson reflected as he sat at the desk and began to eat the breakfast. But then, he thought, undoubtedly all these middle-aged men were preoccupied with their own little pastimes and above all, with the none too pleasing prospect of returning to surgery. Besides, they were in a sense a collection of misfits and failures—like himself—and they could hardly be expected to possess the kind of fraternal *esprit de corps* which would lead them to hail a new member warmly. In any event, they were certainly a resigned and withdrawn lot, he thought. No wonder he had mistaken them for clerks before.

The breakfast, at least, was satisfying. He finished every scrap of bacon and toast, and while waiting for someone to give him instructions—if indeed he was supposed to do anything other than sit where he was—he idly began to pull open the drawers of the desk. There was a variety of items inside: a book of crossword puzzles, some of which had been worked; several large and complicated jigsaw puzzles; a dictionary; a miniature chess set, and pads of yellow ruled paper with an assortment of pencils, some new and unsharpened, others mere stubs bearing teeth-marks.

Feeling disinclined simply to sit unemployed at the desk, while all the other clients were engaged in their little occupations, Wilson took out one of the yellow pads with the idea of doing some sketches to while away the time. The top page was partly torn. He removed it, and underneath discovered a few lines of neat handwriting.

"Being of sound mind and body," the writing began, "I . . ." And at this point were listed several names, each one being crossed out, as if the author had been unable to decide which one to use, and finally, as further testimony to his frustration, the writing ended abruptly with the phrase: "I have nothing to bequeath."

Wilson put the pad away, feeling that he had inadvertently trespassed on the privacy of the gentleman who had formerly used the desk, whose rather eccentric jottings had presumably been overlooked when he had been taken to surgery and his desk cleaned out for the next occupant.

He withdrew instead one of the jigsaw puzzles, and was half-heartedly preparing to assemble it when he realized that one of the other men was slowly approaching him. He glanced up; the man's face was not familiar, not familiar at all, and yet Wilson had the uncanny sensation that he did in fact know who he was, and that on top of this, the face that now was presenting itself was none other than the one he had glimpsed in this same room months before, which at the time had had a chilling effect. Possibly it was the eyes. Great mournful eyes they were, gazing directly into his own with a lugubrious, knowing look.

"How do you do?" Wilson remarked uneasily, rising from his chair.

"Hello, Wilson." The voice was decidedly familiar. Wilson, experiencing a mild rush of vertigo, sat down suddenly. The newcomer drew up another chair, sitting quite close, as if to indicate that their conversation should be guarded, although actually the other men seemed to be paying no attention to them, but continued their chess games and other sedentary activities as before.

"You're Charley," Wilson said, accusingly.

Charley shrugged his shoulders and smiled with a corner of his mouth.

"What are you doing here?" Wilson asked, still bewildered by the sight of those well-remembered eyes set in a strange arrangement of features.

"The same as yourself," said Charley. "Waiting." He chuckled, but without mirth. "You're not a bad-looking fellow now, old boy," he added. "They did a nice job on you. It's a shame it didn't work out."

Wilson wiped his forehead with his sleeve. The huge room seemed to have become uncomfortably warm and close. There were too many men there, sealed up together; it was oppressive. He became aware of the countless little sounds: the mumble of conversation, the turning of pages, and even the whisper of chessmen being shifted to new positions. He found that his own fingers were toying with the jigsaw pieces, which he was aimlessly studying.

"You'd rather not look at me just now, I suppose," said Charley. "Don't worry. I quite understand."

"It's just that it's—it's a bit odd to recognize someone and not to recognize them, at the same time."

"You'll get used to it, Wilson. *I'm* used to it. Your face doesn't bother me the least bit," said Charley, comfortingly, "and in a few days or so you'll find yourself much more at ease. Actually, you'll get to like the place."

Wilson continued to work on the puzzle. "I hope so. I'm sure I will, I mean."

"It's not bad," Charley went on. "The food is good, the accommodations are adequate, and there are all sorts of things to do to pass the time. If you happen to play chess—you did play once, didn't you?—there are several men here who'll be glad to give you a contest. Checkers, too. And other games, of course. Plenty of things while you're waiting."

"Waiting for surgery? Is it awfully crowded, then?"

"For example, I've made a kind of project out of stamp-collecting. Come over to my desk sometime. I'll show you my albums. I've got thirty of them, jam-packed with stamps from every country in the world, and some of them darned rare, too. There's a Nigerian issue, for instance, that's got a peculiar sort of perforation error that exists in only a couple of hundred. Before they changed it, you see. I got that one just last month."

Wilson wiped his brow once more. The box to the

jigsaw puzzle depicted a horse race, but he was having difficulty in finding any piece that remotely resembled part of a horse. He wondered whether the previous occupant of the desk had not put the puzzles away in the wrong boxes.

He ventured a quick glance at Charley. "Excuse me, but how long have you been here?"

"Oh, quite a little while. It's not easy to assemble thirty stamp albums."

"But . . . you were here in this room when I came last year."

"Um, yes."

"And when you telephoned me, you were here then, too?"

"In the building, that's right."

"But good Lord, Charley. Does a man have to wait that long to go back into surgery?"

"Oh, I'm one of the exceptions," Charley said quickly. "I was on a kind of special detail, you see, as your sponsor."

"I don't understand."

"Well, I was asked to sort of stay around so I could telephone you if necessary from time to time. Which I did, as you know. But now . . ." He hesitated.

"But now it won't be necessary," Wilson said. "Well, I can only say I'm truly sorry if I kept you from getting back on the surgery list. I mean, keeping you here all that extra time. But I appreciate it, Charley."

"Don't mention it." Charley sighed. "After all, I was the one who called you in the first place."

"You called from here then, too?"

"Yes."

"But dammit, Charley, when you called that first time, you sounded like the whole experience was something tremendous. Rebirth. And all the time you were here, right here back at the company. Which means, unless I am greatly mistaken, that you yourself had been somewhat short of a success on your first try."

"Well, I guess I thought you'd have a better chance. I figured I was doing you a favor."

"You were, Charley. Believe me, you've been right all the way through this thing. It's my fault that I wasn't able to take proper advantage of it. What you said about pioneering, for example. That hits the question right on the nose, in my judgment. I'm just sorry I couldn't quite live up to the standard on my first time around, and I guess it's been something of a worry to you, watching me take the wrong turn time after time, in spite of all your advice." Charley was silent, and Wilson went on fumbling with the puzzle, which still resisted his efforts to bring it into some kind of order.

"I suppose you knew I'd be a flop from the time I went to Denver, didn't you?" he remarked finally.

"I was afraid you would be. I—I sort of resigned myself to it, though."

Wilson looked up again and saw that Charley's eyes were moist. "Well," he stammered, touched by his friend's show of emotion, "it's damned kind of you . . . really fine, I mean, to be so . . ." He cleared his throat. "And all for my sake, old man. Really, damned unselfish of you."

Charley looked away.

"I must say," Wilson went on, anxious not to evoke any further evidence of distress on Charley's part, "I won't make the same mistakes again!" He produced a rueful chuckle. "You know, Charley, when I got home yesterday, I found Emily'd turned the house upside down. Knocked out my entire study, to make a dining room extension. That was a hell of a shock, I can tell you. And she'd redone the whole house, too—painting, furniture, everything, and there was hardly a trace left—"

He was interrupted by the ringing of a bell. It was not loud, but the sound appeared to have some special meaning for the clients, for at once the conversations were hushed, and the hands that held the chess-pieces stopped in place. Charley had made a quick little movement of his head. He was looking at the door at the front of the room, as indeed were all of the other clients, and so Wilson, too, glanced that way, in time to see the door open to admit two white-clad orderlies and the resident physician with the scarred face.

The doctor stood surveying the silent room and then remarked: "Good morning, gentlemen," and without any further ceremony enunciated two names: "Parker, please, and Walsh," whereupon two of the clients rose from their chairs, shuffled forward, and accompanied by the orderlies, left the room. The doctor remained for only a moment. "Sorry to disappoint the rest of you gentlemen," he declared, "but perhaps tomorrow, eh?" and with his crooked little grin, he, too, turned and walked out.

As the door closed behind him, the customary hum of mild activity resumed within the room; no one seemed to consider the departure of Messrs. Parker and Walsh as anything but a routine occurrence.

"Where did they go, Charley?" Wilson asked.

"To surgery."

"Well, my God. Then they won't be coming back."

"No."

"Well, I must say there was certainly a minimum of leave-taking. You'd think they were just going out to the men's room. Don't people even shake hands with their neighbors around here?"

Charley scratched himself under the arms. "Well, as a matter of fact, it doesn't seem to be the custom. Things go pretty much by the book in this organization, Wilson. I guess you haven't gotten your briefing yet, but the story is simple. Your turn comes and you just go, that's all. They don't waste much time on ceremonies."

"But don't you know when it's your turn? Take yourself. Aren't you on a waiting list now?"

"It doesn't work that way, Wilson. It's not on a list basis."

"Well, how long was Parker here, for instance?"

"A week."

"And Walsh?"

"Oh, about four months."

"But it doesn't seem fair for Parker to get such quick service, when there must be dozens of others who've been waiting longer."

"I don't suppose they really mind."

"Well, it's a pretty passive bunch, I must say. What about you, Charley? Aren't you anxious to be called?"

"Sometimes." However, Charley seemed disinclined to pursue the subject further, and rose from his chair. "You never know, from day to day," he added, "and it helps if you don't much care when it is."

"You mean that you could have been called today?"

Charley shrugged. "Yes, I guess so."

"But—"

"Time for me to get back to my albums, Wilson. See you around."

The days passed slowly. Each was exactly like any other. In the mornings, the clients rose and dressed, and straggled out of their cubicles and along the corridor to the enormous room, where they picked up trays and helped themselves to breakfast dishes that were contained in a large mobile serving table, which attendants wheeled in at mealtimes. Then the men returned to their desks to eat in solitary fashion, following which they resumed their various occupations.

Even the daily sounding of the bell and the appearance of the doctor and orderlies began to take on, in Wilson's mind, a routine aspect. No one else seemed to be awaiting this portentous event with any particular interest; there were no eager, hopeful glances toward the door in anticipation of the bell, and similarly, after the medical party had come and departed with the surgical nominees of the day; there was no babble of commentary among the men who had failed to be chosen. Wilson decided that this apparent lack of interest was a quiet sensible self-discipline, for clearly it would do no good for the clients to become overly concerned about the matter—for example, to the point of organizing a committee to demand that a definite list be followed, to place the system on a basis of strict fairness—because obviously the company would not countenance any changes in an arrangement that was undoubtedly established for excellent reasons. And besides, he found that he himself was falling readily into the mood of the group; he did not especially care about the bell, or the orderlies, or even the doctor. His project of sorting out and matching properly the pieces of the jigsaw puzzles seemed to be far more important than the question of who was called away to surgery, and who arrived as newcomers—and there were two or three each day—to take the vacated places.

He visited Charley's desk occasionally, but found that his old friend seemed to have no concern other than his stamp collection, which Wilson thought boring, certainly when compared to his own effort to straighten out the jigsaw situation, and so, as if by a tacit consent, they came to have little to do with each other.

Once Wilson asked him: "I suppose they give us tranquilizers, don't you think? In the food?"

"Well, if they do, then it's probably for our own good."

"I don't mean to disagree," Wilson said. "After all, you can't have a large group of men living in close quarters like this without something of that sort."

"Probably not. Um, would you mind moving your hand a bit, Wilson? You're on my Southern Rhodesian page, and there are some pretty expensive items there . . ."

Only once did anything out of the ordinary occur, and this was treated by everyone as being the kind of embarrassment that would quickly be forgotten, if acknowledgment were sternly refused. One of the men called by the doctor did not rise, but remained at his desk working on his project, the construction of a sailing ship inside a glass bottle, and when the name was repeated, in a louder voice, he glanced up in annoyance, muttering something. Being called a third time, he did leave his desk, but carried the bottle with him, and when the doctor advised him that he must leave it behind, he became suddenly enraged, smashed the bottle on the floor, and burst inexplicably into tears. The orderlies quickly hustled him from the room, while the doctor surveyed the seated clients with a watchful and sardonic gaze until he was satisfied that this outrageous behavior had been, quite properly, ignored.

A week to the day after Wilson had arrived, he was led away by an attendant for what Charley had termed his briefing. At first Wilson had awaited this event with

impatience, for he assumed it was a necessary preliminary to his being summoned to the surgery, but when
the time came and he actually was being conducted
down a series of passageways toward the briefing
rooms, he found that he was rather irked to have his
work on the puzzles interrupted for some bureaucratic
procedure which, in all likelihood, was not absolutely
necessary.

Nevertheless, he made no complaint, but went
into the briefing office and sat patiently waiting while
the officer in charge thumbed through a small stack
of files, sharpened some pencils, and otherwise completed his little preparations for the briefing.

"My name is Dr. Redfield," the officer remarked
at length, in a pleasant voice. "Ph.D.," he added, with
a deprecatory chuckle, smoothing his tie, and giving
Wilson a disarming glance of modesty. "In history," he
went on cheerfully, as if this were essential for Wilson
to know.

Wilson smiled politely.

"Now," Dr. Redfield declared, "first of all, let me ask
you whether you're in any position to recommend and
sponsor a new client."

"A new client?"

"Yes. Someone in your acquaintance outside who
you feel would benefit by the company's services. You
yourself were sponsored, you know."

"Yes, of course. I see." Wilson frowned down at
his hands, trying to think of someone who might be
a candidate. "Excuse me," he asked, "but if I did spon-

sor someone, would that possibly delay my own trip to surgery? In the event I were needed from time to time to advise him, say?"

"Quite right," said Dr. Redfield briskly. "That indeed would be possible." He chuckled. "That'd give you some extra time to finish that little puzzle project of yours, now wouldn't it?"

Wilson managed to smile, but he decided all at once that he did not particularly care for Dr. Redfield. The man's head was too large and too bald, for one thing, and he kept fiddling with his spectacles—swinging them on one finger, polishing them carelessly on his sleeve—which was most distracting. And besides, it was none of Dr. Redfield's business how Wilson occupied his time.

"Well, I'm sorry," Wilson replied, finally. "I don't seem to be able to think of a single soul."

Dr. Redfield gave him a sharp glance, somewhat at variance with his previous manner of good humor. "Well, Mr. Wilson, that's too bad. That's a shame." He clapped his glasses on his nose and folded his hands firmly. "But perhaps you'll be able to think of someone a bit later on, eh? I mean, names have a way of springing out of thin air, don't they? A business associate, perhaps. Someone who lives down the street, maybe. You don't have to be intimately acquainted with a man, Wilson, to realize that he would be receptive—highly receptive—to the sort of opportunity we offer." He squinted at Wilson severely, as though to suggest that Wilson was deliberately withholding a whole roster of potential clients. "Things may not have worked out to full satisfaction in your case, Wilson," he went on, "but a man must be able to view the situation objectively. By which I mean to say that your own example should not blind you to the fact that others may succeed where you—if you don't mind blunt talk, Wilson—where you have failed." He pressed a button set in a panel on the top of the desk. "As you can imagine," he continued, almost grumpily, "the vast bulk of our new business is acquired through present clients. It's a word-of-mouth operation, Wilson. You don't suppose," he interjected with a hint of sarcasm, "that we can advertise in the magazines and newspapers, do you?"

Two orderlies entered the room and stood awaiting instructions. Dr. Redfield acknowledged their arrival with a petulant wave of one plump hand.

"So I say, Wilson, you'll have time to review your list of friends and acquaintances, and I daresay you'll come up with something, eh?" He grunted, evidently attempting to recapture his original attitude of joviality. "You don't want the company to suffer any further on your account, do you now? Be a good fellow, Wilson, and give us a hand," he persisted, as the orderlies moved a bit closer.

"I'll do my best," Wilson muttered, unable to overcome his aversion to Dr. Redfield. But, thinking it best to conclude their conversation on a more cordial note, he asked: "I'd be interested in knowing what your historical period might be, Doctor."

"The fall of Rome," Dr. Redfield said shortly. "All

right," he told the orderlies, "ready for the next stage," and as Wilson compliantly rose and left with the orderlies, the briefing officer tugged off the spectacles again and shouted after him. "Remember, Wilson. One name is better than none at all!"

The next stage proved to be a medical examination. Wilson was required to remove all of his clothing and submit to the most minute inspection of a fussy young medical technician, who made careful notes and followed what happeared to be an almost interminable checklist. Wilson was poked, prodded, and measured, and then on top of that he was photographed in the nude from a dozen different angles, so that at the end of a half-hour of this kind of treatment, he felt he had the right to ask some questions.

"Excuse me, but I don't quite understand why this is necessary."

"Oh, it's necessary, all right," mumbled the technician, jotting down more notes.

"But I mean as part of a briefing."

"Well, the word 'briefing' may not be too precise, actually. No, not too precise."

"Is this a preliminary to surgery, then?"

"In a sense," replied the technician, still busy with his notes. "For example, to take an extreme case, suppose you'd lost a finger recently. Or a toe. That would be a serious thing."

"Unpleasant, no doubt," said Wilson. "But it wouldn't make all that difference, would it?"

"No difference?" The technician lifted his eyes

from his notes in amazement. "Well, I should think it would. How many clients do you think walk in here who'd also be missing a finger or a toe? And what would be the chances that it would be the *same* finger or toe, hmmm? But of course," he added, returning to his notes, "in your case you have had no such substantial loss since we did our original work on you; merely a few minor changes such as a little fatty tissue here and there, nothing important, but, as you can imagine, everything must be observed and checked and noted down."

"But look here," said Wilson, feeling ill at ease in his nudity beneath the brilliant lights of the examining room, "what have other clients got to do with me? Suppose I had lost a toe. That would be my misfortune, wouldn't it? It wouldn't affect my status with respect to surgery, as far as I can see."

The technician merely shrugged his shoulders, as if he had wasted too much valuable time talking already, and attended even more industriously to his notes.

Wilson was finding the lights almost unbearable. His skin appeared bluish beneath them, and because of the heat, his arms and shoulders were covered with a thin film of moisture. The two muscular young orderlies stood silently behind him, which made him feel even more exposed and uncomfortable. In addition, there was a certain implication in what the technician had said which he did not care for in the slightest.

"I'm sorry to keep repeating myself," he said, as much to break the silence as to obtain information from what quite probably would prove to be an unreliable source, "but this business about fingers and toes is a complete mystery to me. Would you mind explaining it?"

"That's not my job," muttered the technician.

"And what about this tranquilizer dosage? You don't need to pretend it's not a fact," said Wilson, who was beginning to feel decidedly untranquil himself. "What's the purpose of doping us up like cattle, I'd like to know?"

"It avoids unpleasantness," said the technician, at last switching off the powerful photographic lamps and closing up his file folder. He motioned to the orderlies. "Next stage, please."

"What kind of unpleasantness?" asked Wilson anxiously, but the technician had turned away and at the same time the orderlies were gently urging him into his clothing. "We've got to hurry, sir," one of them said. "We don't want to get off schedule." He helped Wilson into the shirt. "There are other gentlemen waiting, you see," he added respectfully.

"Waiting for what?" Wilson grumbled, putting on his slippers, but of course he realized that the orderlies would not be permitted to tell him, even if they wished to do so. "Well, all right," he said. "I'm ready."

He was ushered out of the examining room and into a small adjoining office, where a slender gentleman dressed in a black clerical suit sat composedly behind a desk which was bare except for a prayer book and a statuette of the crucifixion.

"Sit down, please," said the clerical gentleman, rising to indicate a chair on the other side of the desk, and gently dismissing the orderlies. He smiled in a friendly way at Wilson. "You're Parker, I believe."

"Wilson."

"Oh, yes. Parker was last week. But there is a resemblance."

"Excuse me," said Wilson, determinedly, "but I have some questions I'd like—"

"To be sure," said the other man. "That's what I'm here for. Questions." He patted his fingertips benignly together and introduced himself as Dr. Morris. "Let me ask you first, Mr. Wilson, as to your religious preference."

"I have none, as it happens. But I was going to—"

"You were perhaps reared in the Protestant faith?"

"Yes."

"And you were never converted to any other?"

"Well, no."

"Good. That is," Dr. Morris amended with a smile, "I mean 'good' in the sense that we have a certain definition. I don't mean to suggest that being a Protestant is any better than being a Catholic or a Jew, and as a matter of fact, I would be qualified, if I may say so, to serve you in either of those faiths as well."

Wilson gazed at him uncertainly.

"Meaning that I have been ordained," said Dr. Morris modestly, "in each. Rabbi, priest, minister. I admit it's unusual, and perhaps a bit 'advanced,' as you might put it, but on the other hand, the company is anxious to cover as much ground as possible at minimum expense. A praiseworthy attitude, mind you, although it does indicate that at the moment the religious department—meaning my humble self—is perhaps a mite less influential than it will surely become some day. I foresee the time," he declared, "when there will be at least one minister for each faith, Mr. Wilson. With perhaps a department head of sufficient experience," he added, meaningfully, "to exercise adequate supervision."

"Yes, I see," said Wilson. "But as for my questions—"

Dr. Morris ignored the unasked questions. "The workload is already tremendous, Mr. Wilson. Too much for any one man, actually, especially when one has to keep switching back and forth from Gospel to Torah, depending on the client. And then, you can imagine my trepidation, sir, when I consider it is a distinct statistical possibility that one day I may be confronted with a Moslem!" He nodded his head sagely at Wilson. "I've warned them, Mr. Wilson. I've given them plenty of notice. But they merely keep putting me off. 'Budgetary problems.' That's what they say. The unfortunate part is that it's true, I suppose. Corners must be cut. Costs must be reduced. I know that. But at the same time . . ."

Wilson sat stolidly in his chair, hoping that Dr. Morris's complaints would run their course before the orderlies reappeared to hustle him to some other stage of his briefing. From time to time he nodded politely, and muttered civil phrases of agreement, but as the time passed and Dr. Morris showed no signs of reaching a conclusion, his impatience rose up, together with a certain anxiety.

"You must tell me, Dr. Morris," be broke in finally, "what's going to happen to me. I've got to know that."

"What's going to happen to you? Why, my good sir, this is the end of your briefing. No more stages, Mr. Wilson. When we have finished"—the minister glanced at his wristwatch—"then you will be conducted back to the dayroom to rejoin your comrades."

"I don't mean that. I mean . . ." Wilson's voice trailed off. He waved his hands, seeking adequate words. "I mean . . . ultimately."

"Ah," said Dr. Morris, and as if recalled to his professional duties, he composed his features into a more pious expression. "Ultimately, Mr. Wilson. Ultimately, we will be called to face the Creator and render up our last account. It happens to all of us, sir."

"But what about *me*—now?"

"Every mortal man must experience the translation from earthly habitation—"

"That's not an answer!" Wilson's impatience now was almost beyond endurance. He found that his heart was pounding, that his skin was flushed with perspiration, and that his hand had reached out to grasp, as if for support, the statuette on the desk. "You aren't giving me a straight answer, Dr. Morris! You know what I've got to find out!"

"Don't shout, sir, please." Dr. Morris's piety had taken on a coloration of alarm. He smiled placatingly, but his right hand edged stealthily to the corner of the desk, toward a call-button. "Get a grip on yourself, Mr. Wilson. And by the way, that statuette is plastic, sir, and might easily be cracked."

Wilson withdrew his hand. "Please," he asked, in a more controlled voice. "Just answer my question. Only one question, that's all. Don't ring for the orderlies, Dr. Morris, I beg you. Just—"

"All right, Mr. Wilson. It's only that this room is so confoundedly small, and when someone starts shouting, it's sheer bedlam. If the company'd only give me an office of decent size—"

"My question," Wilson said quickly, to forestall another review of administrative shortcomings, "is— what actually happens in what they call surgery?"

"Well, I'm no surgeon, Mr. Wilson. I'm not in attendance on those occasions, sir, as I'm sure you will realize—"

"You're being evasive, Dr. Morris."

"—and I can only advise you," the minister continued, "to make your peace with yourself and your God, whether you happen to have one or not . . ."

Wilson nodded his head. He kept nodding it. The words of Dr. Morris seemed somehow to have become connected with those muscles of his neck which governed nodding, so that each word produced a corresponding little jerking movement of the head.

" . . . 'Our time is a very shadow that passeth away,' " Dr. Morris droned on, quoting with liberality from both Jewish and Christian sources, " 'and man that is born of woman is of few days, and full of trouble . . .'"

As he spoke, the minister kept glancing furtively at his watch, and at the door, occasionally giving Wilson a reassuring smile, and then blinking in an abstracted way around the room, as though even while providing his visitor with divine consolation, he were still preoccupied with the lowly status of the religious department.

"'I am the resurrection and the life; he that believeth in me, though he were, um, dead, yet shall he live . . .'"

Dr. Morris began to speak more hastily, sometimes getting his quotations jumbled, or uttering those that were inappropriate to the occasion, and Wilson's nodding, too, continued at a faster pace. He tried to hold his head still, but in vain. He finally seized his head with his hands, attempting both to stop its movements and to cover his ears. Dr. Morris was right; the office was too small, too terribly small. The walls seemed to lean against each other, separated only by a tiny cushion of air, and the air itself was being sucked away by the vacuum of the minister's voice, so that soon the substance would be quite gone, and there would be nothing to prevent the walls from flopping down on them.

He shouted something at the walls. His eyes were closed, his ears blocked tightly by his hands, his body doubled up in the chair waiting for the room to fold him flat. The only thing to do was shout. Shout for help.

Then he felt something nip at his arm; a single tooth. He looked wildly around.

Dr. Morris had departed. The orderlies had returned, and one of them was holding an empty syringe. But the walls, at least, had not fallen.

"I want to see my contract," Wilson said. "I've got a right to see my contract." He glared at the orderlies, who remained impassive. "It's bound to be in the contract, if it's there—and it couldn't be there because I read it myself." He raised his hands imploringly. "At least, I *think* I read it."

The orderlies gently raised him to his feet and moved him to the door.

"It wasn't exactly a contract, come to think of it," Wilson said. "It was in the form of a will, actually, but a man can't legally will his living body for medical or commercial purposes—it simply can't be done, gentlemen!" The orderlies grunted with the effort of propelling him along the corridor, but made no other response. "It's against the common law! It's against all moral standards! Of course, I realize that the will was made by a man who no longer exists," Wilson added, attempting to anticipate what would undoubtedly be the company's counterarguments, "and that in my present form I am, in a sense, actually a creation of the company, so that possibly there are certain proprietary rights involved . . . But only skin-deep, gentlemen! Only skin-deep! I mean, you can take back the pound of flesh, but the blood—that's mine, isn't it? . . . Isn't it?" he echoed plaintively, as the orderlies carefully conveyed him into a small room and eased him down on an old-fashioned black leather sofa. He tried to rise, but his legs refused to push him up. He stared down at them in perplexity.

"Do you feel calmer, sir?" one of the orderlies inquired, not unkindly.

"Oh—well, yes," said Wilson, truthfully. His arm ached a bit where the needle had gone in, but otherwise he was physically at ease. "It's not a question of calmness, my young friends," he added, "but of justice. Human justice." He sought to describe the shape of justice with his hands, but they, too, declined to obey him, preferring to remain limply folded in his lap, and when he glanced up from them, he discovered that the orderlies had gone.

"Hello, Mr. Wilson."

It was the company president, seated across the little room in a sagging wooden chair.

"I'm sorry—I guess I didn't notice you, sir," said Wilson.

"Not at all," the old man said, with a deprecatory gesture. "I'm not the noticeable type, my boy." He sighed and fumbled with his vest, from which two buttons were missing. "I'm sorry about all of this, Mr. Wilson," he finally said. "I really hoped you'd make it. I hoped you'd find your dream come true."

"I never had a dream."

"Maybe that was it," the old man said. "Yes, that

may very well have been it." He nodded his head in a forlorn way, as if Wilson had provided him with a distressing but inevitable insight.

"I seem to be nothing but trouble for you," Wilson said, humbly. "Coming—and going."

"Ah, well," the old man muttered, scratching his seamed forehead and then inspecting his fingernails. "You're not the only one, my boy."

"You mean all the others in the dayroom?"

"Those, and others. There are other dayrooms, Mr. Wilson. We keep having to add them on, and it's taking up space required for administrative and operating divisions, I'm afraid, but there's not much we can do about it. No sir, the proportion of failures—if you'll forgive the word—is so high, my boy, that I'd be ashamed to mention it to you. But possibly it makes you feel a little better to know that you're not in a minority?"

"Not really."

"No, I suppose not." The president sighed again. His chair creaked sympathetically. "No, it's not a minority, I fear," he repeated, and then, mumbling slightly, he added: "Oh, when I began the business—and that was a long time ago, son, an awfully long time—I was a young man myself . . ." He paused and blew his nose. "Um, what was I saying?"

"You were telling me about when you started the business."

"Yes. Well, I was a young man, as I said. A young man with an idea." He chuckled mournfully. "Believe

me, Mr. Wilson, there's nothing in the world so fright-
ening and pathetic as a young man with an idea! And
an altruistic idea, to boot. That's the worst. No sir, I
wasn't aiming to make a lot of money. It had to be a
self-supporting commercial operation, true enough,
but that was just the necessary foundation to give
expression to this idea of mine. You know: helping
others. Helping others to a little happiness . . . and not
just the wealthy—although at first, of course, I realized that I'd have to start with those who could afford
high fees—but ultimately everybody. A mass market,
Mr. Wilson." He drew out his pipe and rubbed it carefully against his cheek, then began to fill it from an old
leather tobacco pouch.

"Yes?"

"Oh. Well, then the failures began. I didn't pay much
attention at first, you see, being preoccupied with the
administrative end of things. I thought to myself: get
the business established on a firm footing, and then
there'd be time to iron out the bugs. And all the time,
you understand, I took comfort in the thought that in
my small way I was waging a battle against human
misery. I *was*, too, except . . ." He stopped to light his
pipe.

"Except what, sir?"

"Eh? Oh, except that the failures kept on coming,
more and more, and I finally had to admit that I might
possibly have based my enterprise on a fallacy. I've
always tried to be honest with myself, son. That's the
only way to live honorably." He waved his pipe, which

promptly went out, and he was forced to light it again. "As for that fallacy, it was simply this: that my business seemed to attract the wrong kind of clients. In fact, I often wondered whether it didn't attract *only* the wrong kind of clients."

"I don't quite—"

"It's simple, my boy. My clients were men who were ready to abandon their original identities . . . and why? Because, for one reason or another, they had made a botch of things (apart from material success, of course), and I can't imagine what possessed me to think that these gentlemen would be likely to do much better just because I gave them a new face and a new name."

"But if you realized this, then why didn't you stop? I don't mean to be critical," said Wilson, "but wasn't it just a little bit dishonest to keep on?"

The old man looked even sadder than before. "Ah, well, you're right, Wilson. But it wasn't all that easy. By the time I came to this conclusion, you see, I had built up a big organization. I had a staff running into the hundreds. I had a tremendous investment in facilities and equipment and the like, which couldn't just be turned off overnight, you know. And then, too," he added ruefully, "I was no longer the only voice in authority, because we're a modern concern, Wilson, with profit-sharing and a board of directors and all . . ." He put his pipe away again. "And I couldn't very well take sole responsibility for throwing all these people out of work, could I? As it is, Wilson, we're having some financial difficulties. You've got no idea what the expenses are like in this sort of business," he remarked, gloomily. "We keep needing to get more clients to help support the cost of processing those we're working on, and we have to cut all sorts of corners . . . and then, too, we've got to keep a close check on the reborns outside, because with the high incidence of failure, we never can tell when one of them might try to make trouble by, for instance, deciding to sue us in court. You can see why we couldn't let that happen, Wilson."

"Naturally."

"And some *do* make a go of it, my boy." The old man's face brightened. "Not many, but some. That makes it better, doesn't it? And we are working constantly to find ways of improving on that proportion," he added, wistfully. "I may not see it in my lifetime, but the younger executives like Joliffe may, and in fact I believe they will. Oh, you can call it wishful thinking, son, but it all began with a wish, didn't it? And our life is built on wishes. We've got to keep plugging away," the old man declared severely, admonishing Wilson with one bony finger. "We can't just give up. We've got to push on, we've got to stay solvent and reduce costs wherever we can," he said, referring again to his financial troubles. "Why, do you know that up until last year our Cadaver Procurement Section was running thirty and forty percent over budget, sir?"

Wilson stirred uneasily on the sofa. "But you've managed to take care of that problem now," he muttered.

"Yes, yes. We—" The president stopped himself. "Sorry, Wilson. I'm afraid that example was not too aptly chosen, considering your position."

Wilson merely shrugged, or rather, tried to shrug. He seemed to be even more divorced from his body than before, as if it were gradually, by means of the injection, acquiring an independent existence. If it got up and walked away, he wondered, would he remain in the little room . . . and if he did, what would he consist of?

"Could you do it now—right now?" he asked, although he did not particularly care.

"Do what? Oh—well, no, Wilson. That's impossible. We have to wait until a client appears who answers your general measurements."

"But what about cold storage?"

"I'm afraid that's full-up, my boy. Anyway, we've found that we get the best results on the alternative basis. Cheaper, too. Less surgical conditioning."

"I see," Wilson said, or thought he said. He was not sure that his lips had moved, nor was he positive that he had heard his words, for the disembodied sensation was growing stronger, and it seemed that the power of speech and hearing was in a process of erosion. Sight, too, was becoming somewhat uncertain. The old man across the room was nothing more than a thin little shadow now, and his reedy voice was subject to irregular fluctuations, as if it were governed by a spluttering radio tube about to expire absolutely. Only phrases here and there came through with clarity.

" . . . look at it this way, my boy . . . Opportunity for someone else . . . make amends for your failure . . ."

The dim overhead light now seemed to be slowly splitting into fragments, tiny points of light which danced in the air, then gradually became fixed in space.

Still the old man's voice continued, fitfully:

"It's your immortality, in a way, my boy . . . When most men die, they just die, that's all, without a purpose . . ."

Now the points of light were being extinguished, one by one. There was only darkness behind them.

" . . . but for you, there'd be a purpose. Giving someone else a chance. Isn't that better than . . . ? Isn't that the point of life, my boy . . . ?"

Only a few of the lights remained.

"Love," whispered the unsteady old voice. "It's love, son, the only kind of love that counts . . . Unselfish love . . ."

Now there were but two lights, and these so shrunken and uncertain that their existence seemed in doubt. He thought he might as well make one last effort to speak before they, too, faded into darkness together with the old man, the room, the building, city, everything; and so, swiftly but carefully choosing his words, he delivered a final response.

"It really doesn't matter," he said.

ABOUT THE AUTHOR

DAVID ELY was born in Chicago and was educated at the University of North Carolina, Harvard, and Oxford. He is a former newspaperman and the author of seven novels and two collections of short stories. His novel *Seconds* was the basis for the 1966 Rock Hudson film of the same title. He and his wife live on Cape Cod, in Massachusetts.